The Gnomes' Rosette

Tales of Limindoor Woods

by Sieglinde De Francesca

• Book 3 •

To my Grandchildren &
to all Children & their Parents
& to Everyone Else

Also by Sieglinde De Francesca

༄ Books for Children ༄

A Donsy of Gnomes: 7 gentle gnome stories

The Way of Gnome: Tales of Limindoor Woods, book 1

Gnomes & Friends: Tales of Limindoor Woods, book 2

༄ Books for Grown-ups ༄

The Guilds of Tir na nÓg: A Collection of Celtic Dream Tales

Teaching with the Fables: a holistic approach

Coloring with Block Crayons: a manual of coloring techniques

Jacket design & text decorations by the author

© S. De Francesca 2017   ♦   All rights reserved.

No part of this book may be reproduced in any way without written permission from the author. Please ask for permission, she will most likely give it.

teachwonderment.com

ISBN 978-1-5323-3892-2

Contents

The World of Gnomes 5

An Important Notice 7

Map of Limindoor Woods 11

The Gnomes' Rosette 13

   1. Autumn 15
   2. The Cycle of Life 19
   3. A Passing 22
   4. The Festival 32
   5. The Feast 39
   6. A Story 45
   7. Gratitude 53
   8. Thanks 58
   9. Rosette 61
  10. A Fright 66
  11. A New Home 72
  12. New Friends 77
  13. More Gifts 83
  14. The Explorers 92
  15. Muddy Brook 99
  16. A Song 107

17.	A Gift	117
18.	A Dream	124
19.	The Builders	131
20.	The Bridge	136
21.	Uh, oh!	141
22.	The Offering	151
23.	A Request	163
24.	Catsa	169
25.	The Climb	178
26.	The Song	184
27.	Good News	191
28.	The Guardian	195
29.	Autumn's End	201
30.	Winter	209

Things to Ponder 219

About the Author 238

In Gratitude 241

The World of Gnomes

The world of gnome is ephemeral. You must cross a threshold to enter there. That threshold is barely more than an opening in the mist.

You are most likely to find the way there when you are out among the wonders of nature, particularly in an old, old forest.

~ *A Donsy of Gnomes,* S. De Francesca

Limindoor Woods has long been a haven for a number of gnomes who found refuge there from the ever encroaching outside world of humans, or Tall Ones.

The name Limindoor is a combination of the word *limen* meaning threshold and *door* as in access. For indeed those woods are embraced by a unique and magical perimeter.

In these chapters, you will encounter a whole donsy or gathering of gnomes and their friends, both animal, and human — who are from both in and around that enchanted forest.

It is my belief that stories are gifts. They are meant to be shared, told or read - by and to - both children and adults. They are meant for the delight and education of all.

These are stories to curl up with; to enjoy at bedtime, outdoors, or by the fireplace. They are stories to think about, to talk about, stories to dream on.

The tales that began in *The Way of Gnome* and *Gnomes and Friends* continue here with *The Gnomes' Rosette*.

An Important Notice to Parents & Guardians

As you have the primary role in choosing what stories you share with your children, you should be aware that in this book there is news of a *death* that had recently happened in Limindoor Woods.

Whenever I sit down and open myself to writing about the special world of these gnomes I feel that I am "given" these stories.

Even before I knew the subject of this book, I was led to write about, what is to most people, a very delicate subject … the death of a loved one.

In this case, it is the death of an animal, a talking animal, an animal whom the children who have read the previous Limindoor books have grown to love: Mees, the mouse.

Having had children of my own, and now being blessed with four grandchildren, I am aware of how important it is to address this subject with sensitivity, respect and honesty. I have striven to do so here.

By identifying death's role in the 'Cycle of Life' you can perhaps help your child come to a deeper understanding of it.

My hope is that the events written here might in some way help your child. That your child will find a sense of understanding and peace, when the time inevitably comes that they experience the loss of a loved one; a pet, a friend or a relative.

Furthermore, dear parent or guardian, I request or at least suggest, that you first, *to yourself,* read through pages 19-31 so you may be prepared for any questions your child might ask.

For those children who *did* have a fondness for Mees the mouse and are pained by his loss, I recommend that when comforting your child you take some time to talk about their favorite memories of Mees – and to discuss any feelings they might be experiencing.

And, when the time is right, you can remind them that, by reading further in this book, they will discover many *new* wonders in Limindoor Woods. And that they might make a brand new special friend here as well.

If you find that there is a discrepancy between the traditions you are familiar with, concerning death, and the traditions you read about here, perhaps it would be best to remember that different cultures have different beliefs. The traditions you read of here are simply how 'the gnomes do it.'

With that, I wish you all a pleasant journey as you continue your adventures with the Gentle-gnomes and their friends in Limindoor Woods.

Map of Limindoor Woods

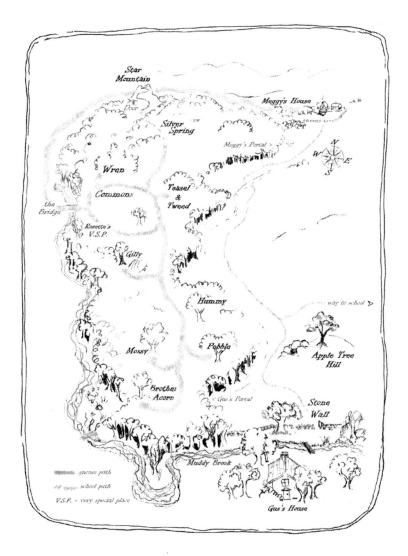

The Gnomes' Rosette

Tales of Limindoor Woods

1.
Autumn

Autumn had come to the land and had joyously scattered its glorious sunset colors all over the countryside. Everywhere the leaves were the colors of gold and flame - throughout Limindoor Woods and for miles beyond.

There are many grand, old-growth trees that make up the secret forest that is Limindoor Woods. A happy, gurgling brook winds around two sides of it. And a steep mountain, mysteriously *un*seen by almost everyone outside of Limindoor, rises in the north of the woods. Near the middle of the forest is an open grassy field known as the Commons.

Although rolling farmlands border on three sides of the forest there is no easy entrance into it; for much of the tree-line is bound with a densely tangled thicket of bracken and prickly undergrowth.

Just that last summer Gus and Meggy had become two of the luckiest children you can imagine. They and they alone were the *only* children of Tall Ones (that means children like you) who had ever found their way *into* the magic of Limindoor Woods. And when inside the woods, they found that, they had become surprisingly *very small* – as small as the Gentle-gnomes they met and befriended there.

But then, all too soon, their splendid free summer days were over. When autumn arrived the children had to spend their weekdays in a one-room school house – a place that is half an hour's walk east of their homes. And only on the weekends, only after doing their chores at home, could they once again crawl through the magic portal into Limindoor Woods to visit their friends there.

It is good to be aware, Dear Reader, that the events in this story took place a long time ago. It was the time when your grandparents, or maybe even *their* grandparents, were young. Their world was such a different place then, in so many ways.

No matter the season, most people who lived in those times, children and adults alike, were always busy. Every day there were tasks to do, indoors and out. Wood had to be chopped, food had to be prepared, cleaning had to be done, gardens had to be tended, horses had to be cared for and hens to be fed - all of this and more had to be done every day.

Likewise, there was much work for the gnomes of Limindoor Woods to do, particularly with winter so close.

Had you been there, you would have seen many busy gnomes shuffling through the crisp fallen leaves, breathing little puffs of fog, diligently preparing for the coming months.

Each gnome had a task to do to contribute to their community.

There was food to store for the cold months; fruits and vegetables, seeds and nuts. And there was firewood and moss to gather, as well as warm clothes to get ready before the snows came.

Those first nippy winds that danced around the treetops and across the Commons of Limindoor Woods foretold many changes.

2.
The Cycle of Life

However, Dear Reader, before we continue further with our story, there is something important that you must know. Something very sad has happened in Limindoor.

The wise and kind field-mouse, who was Mossy the Gnome's good friend, has died.

His name was Mees. He had lived with Mossy and was greatly loved by everyone in Limindoor for many *long mouse-years*.

Actually, Mees had already reached a very ripe old age for mice. In fact, even then, he was much older than what would equal *a hundred* of our human years!

When his friend Mossy the Gnome had first come to Limindoor Woods, many, many years before, he had made the acquaintance of *another* field-mouse whose name was Mus – (later known as Mus the First). Mossy and Mus had become such great friends that they had decided to live together.

Mus remained as Mossy's companion for the rest of *his* mouse-life. When he was gone, (another way to say that 'he died,') one of Mus's relatives found his way to Mossy's door to become his *new* companion. And so that story repeated, over and over again. And it had been that way for a very, very long time.

Please understand, Dear Reader, that this is a part of the way of things in the Natural World. Birth and growth and eventually death are all part of the wonderful thing called the 'Cycle of Life.'

The day always becomes night and then is reborn again in the morning. Seasons change from warm to cold and back again. Trees grow green leaves in the spring. Those leaves thrive in the sunshine, wind, and rain of summer and, in the autumn the colors of the leaves change to reds, golds, and browns. Then before winter, they fall and blanket the ground. Eventually, they become part of the earth again – only to be taken up by the tree's roots to nourish the tree - so it can grow more leaves. And so the cycle continues.

Our dear Mees knew what was happening. Any mouse who had lived as many *long mouse-years* as he had, had become very wise. He knew well that it would soon be time for him to depart.

3.
A Passing

Here is what happened. One still evening, near the end of the summer, Mossy was sitting as usual on his bench, enjoying his pipe of Bearberry bark. And his friend Mees lay his feet.

After a while, Mees reached up and placed his paw on Mossy's knee and said, "Mossy... Mossy, the time for me to leave is coming soon."

The old gnome lovingly regarded the mouse for a moment before quietly saying, with a catch in his voice, "Oh, Mees! Are you sure?"

"It will be alright, Mossy. You know that it will."

Then he added, "I have been so *happy* living here and so *happy* to have you as my friend."

"I feel the same way, Mees. You have been such a great companion. Oh, Mees, I shall miss you!" said Mossy warmly clasping Mees's delicate paw in his stubby hand.

They sat like that for some time until Mossy asked, "What would you like to do, Mees? Are you up to visiting all of your friends in Limindoor? Or would you prefer that they come here?"

Mees thought about it for a while and finally said, "I think I would like them to come here, Mossy, if that is alright with you."

"Certainly, certainly it is. We will ask Hummy Bee to tell all of our friends the first thing tomorrow."

The next day Hummy had been so busy all morning spreading the news that Mossy's garden was soon crowded with all of Mees's gnome and animal friends.

Fortunately, Pebble had just returned from caring for the crystals in his cave and hadn't gone to sleep yet - so he was able to come.

Even the two children, Meggy and Gus, were there.

Hummy had had to fly *outside* of Limindoor to find the children who were sitting up in the tree atop of Apple Tree Hill. Of course, since they were outside of Limindoor, they were *full sized* children. But they recognized each other right away. That's what friends do. So, even without being able to understand what Hummy was saying, they promptly followed her to Mossy's house.

Well, it could have been a very sad occasion with everyone there saying goodbye to their friend for the last time. But this was Limindoor where the gnomes wisely followed 'The Way of Gnome.'

For those of you who don't know, 'The Way' is a guide on how to become a Gentle-gnome. It is also known as the 'Golden Rules of Gnome'. (You can read about this at the back of this book on page 221.)

But, for now, you need only to know that *Celebrations* are very important to the gnomes. So, instead of them all being a gloomy lot standing around Mossy's yard and feeling sad about Mees's departure, they followed the Gentle-gnome Way and turned it into a Celebration - a Celebration of their *love* for Mees.

One way they showed their love for him was by sharing stories of some of the favorite times they'd spent with their mouse friend.

Teasel was the first one to speak up.

"Mees, I remember you once telling us that you had seen a *fairy*. I believe you said that Hummy was chatting with her just before the fairy disappeared inside a blossom. How fortunate you were to have seen that! I, myself, have never seen a fairy!"

Many in the group smiled and nodded in agreement with him, for there were few gnomes who *had* ever seen a fairy.

And Tweed added, "And, I recall you saying that that fairy was quite 'extraordinarily enchanting,' and very 'diminutive'. Oh, Mees, you always do like those big words, don't you?" (By the way, Reader, 'diminutive' means tiny).

"It's true, I have always been rather fond of 'elaborate terminology'," agreed Mees chuckling along with everyone else.

"As I recall, you have always loved being scratched behind your ears, haven't you?" said Wren as she stepped towards him and gave his velvety ears loving strokes.

"Ah, thank you, Wren, that was lovely," purred Mees. (Reader, did you know that mice purred?)

Gus, not being a *real* gnome, was having a very difficult time with the idea of having to say a "last goodbye" to Mees.

But after sensing the *love* that everyone in the group was feeling, he thought he would share something too.

"You know, Mees," he said a bit shyly. "You and Mossy were the first ones I saw when I first came to Limindoor Woods. I was such a silly – I thought you were Mossy's *dog*! I didn't know at the time that *I* had become *gnome-sized*."

Even though only some gnomes knew what dogs were, they understood how confused Gus must have been. Everyone laughed kindly along with Gus when he shared how puzzled he was to discover Mees was a *mouse*.

"And, I also remember one of the first things you said to me, Mees," Gus continued as he started feeling more comfortable about sharing.

"You said, "Everything will be alright." You said that I "should stay and meet the gnomes of Limindoor Woods" - that "they were really very nice, every one of them.""

"And you were right, you know. They are so nice! So I did stay. And I am so, so glad that I did," he said looking around him with a grin.

"We are glad you did, too!" the gnomes and mouse all chorused in.

"I remember how much you enjoy my mama's Apple Jackets, Mees," said Meggy as she timidly stepped forward. "Oh… I *am* sorry I didn't bring you one today. I mean, I didn't know…" she added starting to tear up.

"That's right," added Gus as he went to Meggy's side. He knew how uncomfortable she was and wanted to lighten the mood. "You always have had *such* a good appetite, Mees!"

The crowd laughed heartily at that: for indeed Mees could certainly eat a lot - for a field-mouse that is.

Mossy stepped forward and said, "I wish to share something I remember Mees once saying to our friend Gus here.

It was that time when Gus was so sad about Mr. Twigwhittle going away.

"Mees, I recall you suggesting to Gus, "Why not just wish him well on his journey?""

(Mr. Twigwhittle was a kind old gnome who had come to Limindoor that summer, befriended Gus and then surprisingly just went away, without even saying goodbye.)

There was silence in the group then, while everyone thought about what he had said –

"Why not just wish him well on his journey?"

Realizing that there really was nothing else to say after that, Brother Acorn started to hum. It was a song they all loved, called "Make New Friends."

(Reader, you can find the music for this song on page 224.)

Soon they all joined in singing it - Mees as well.

Make new friends, but keep the old.
Some are silver, and the others gold.
A circle is round, it has no end.
That's how long, we will all be friends.

                        - Anonymous

After the song, there was laughter and, yes, perhaps some tears, but it was all in the spirit of Celebration and Gratitude and Love.

With the goodbyes all said and their friends having gone home, Mossy and Mees had one last evening to share together.

There they sat in the silence of the woods; hand in paw, looking up at the stars that glimmered through the treetops above. Mossy puffed on his Bearberry pipe - a curl of sweet woodsy smoke rising above him.

The last thing he said to Mees was, "I thank you, good friend."

"And, thank you, dear Mossy," Mees replied.

Mees was given back to the earth in a sunny clearing that lay little south of Mossy's home.

Over the next few days, each gnome came to where he was buried. There they paused, thanked him for being such a good mouse friend and left him a bouquet of colorful autumn leaves.

Soon his grave was all a splendor with the colors of autumn.

4.
The Festival

All of the events that you just heard about had happened weeks before.

Of course, all the gnomes still carried thoughts and memories of Mees close in their hearts and they would do so for a long time yet.

When anyone felt sad about Mees's passing, they had only to think of a happy memory of him or something they loved about him, and they would smile. And if they could, they would share the thought with whoever was nearby.

Time moved on. The coming season would not wait. As the weather got colder - winter had to be prepared for.

Also, the gnomes knew that it was almost the time for a very special event - the Gnomes' Thanks-Giving Celebration!

Every year at that time, the good gnomes of Limindoor Woods would gather to celebrate all the things that they were grateful for.

Tradition decreed that their Gnomes' Thanks-Giving Celebration must be a magnificent event! They could always count on there being good food and music, stories and sometimes even *magic*. For Mother Comfrey, their beloved Healing Gnome always returned to Limindoor to be the Mistress of Ceremonies for the festival.

Oh, such preparations they would make in order that the festival would be just perfect! The meadow they called the Commons was completely transformed.

Gnomes placed creek stones in a large circle in the middle of the field. Then they stacked kindling and branches inside the circle in preparation for the festival's bonfire.

Gaily colored fallen leaves were then raked into a mound around that circle for the gnomes to sit on.

The Ding-Dong, polished till it shone bright silver, was readied to proclaim the start of the festival.

Some of you will recall that the Ding-Dong was a mysterious object that had been discovered at the roots of a fallen tree. Gus believed it was a Tall One's *key* and he was pretty sure that he knew what the key went to. But, as the gnomes were neither familiar with keys, nor with the idea of locking things away, they were more interested in finding another use for the object. So Mossy decided that it would make a fine gong, or Ding-Dong, to be hung in the Commons and be rung to announce special events. And there it hangs.

As no festival is complete without food, you can be sure there were many preparations being done in that department.

Traditionally, a delicious Gratitude Soup was served at the festival. It was a soup that *everyone* contributed to.

Do you know the old story of 'Stone Soup?' It's a folk tale about a hungry stranger who comes to a village and convinces each person there to contribute a small portion of their food to go into a soup pot, in order to make a meal for everyone to enjoy.

Well, the gnomes' Gratitude Soup is much like Stone Soup. Each gnome brings some foodstuff to add to a large pot and then, with water, heat from the fire, patience, and everyone's gratitude, it turns into a delicious soup for all to share.

The soup is started with a large pot of fresh water from Muddy Brook (That is the name of the brook that runs around part of Limindoor. Its water is really very *clear*, though.) Then the gnomes contribute vegetables from Gilly's garden, herbs from the meadow, roots and mushrooms from the forest. (They know, of course, to pick *only the right kinds* of mushrooms!)

If any of you are wondering where they got the pot that the soup was cooked in, they had Mother Comfrey to thank for that.

She was famous for finding lost or discarded things from the Tall Ones' world.

You see, the pot was nothing other than a baby Tall One's silver drinking cup that the old gnome had found in her travels.

In the olden times, which are when these tales take place, it was often the tradition in the Tall One's world, for newborn babies to be given their very own, small, *silver* drinking cup. And just as often, the child's name would be engraved on its side. In this case, Mother Comfrey's soup pot had the name 'Emma' on it.

Fortunately, Gus's and Meggy's parents had permitted the children to remain in the woods until *after* sundown, for the special event. It had become clear, by then, to both families that the children knew their way around the woods very well and would be perfectly safe there.

And, as they had been told that there was to be a Gnomes' Thanks-Giving

Celebration in the woods, both of the children's mamas had offered to help bake something yummy. This might be the children's first Limindoor Gnomes' Thanks-Giving Celebration - but they would *not* be coming empty handed!

Gus and Meggy, you see, were both quite famous in Limindoor for the delicious baked goods they brought from home. Those gnomes surely did *love* their bread and pastries!

Wren had been practicing a new tune on her flute - one that she had recently learned from a wood-thrush. She couldn't wait to share it with her friends.

Brother Acorn had checked and rechecked his basket of acorn cups to be sure that they were clean and that there were enough for everybody. He even included several walnut-shell bowls for those gnomes with large appetites.

Brother Acorn and Hummy, along with help from Teasel and Tweed, had prepared a collection of bees-wax acorn-cap candles to be handed out at the end of the festival to light everyone's way home. (If you wish to make some of your own, Reader, the instructions can be found on page 234.)

Pebble had helped Gilly move the long plank of bark they always used for a table top into the Commons and rested it across two wood stumps.

After the table was decorated with an arrangement of colored leaves, various baked goods were laid out on it. Two delicate bowls, fashioned from discarded egg shells, were filled with some of Hummy's delicious honey and were placed at each end of the table. There were also nests of moss, filled with pieces of late harvested fruit on the table for the enjoyment of all.

How lovely everything looked!

5.
The Feast

A great 'Clang! Clang' sounded out as Mossy struck the Ding-Dong!

The Celebration had begun!

Everyone, even the animals, had gathered from near and far. There were Red, Brown and Grey Squirrel families with their young. Yes, beloved Gri-Gri was there, too. Hummy the Bee and some of her sisters, Old Hibou the owl, several rabbits, Mr. Fox (who remembered his manners), a very timid Lady Doe, and a chorus of happy birds, including the well-loved Master Kruk the crow, all gathered about when they heard the gong.

Then, as if on cue, in rode Mother Comfrey.

Perhaps, Reader, this is a good time to remind you about Mother Comfrey. Mother Comfrey is a very special gnome. She serves as a healer for all of Limindoor Woods and the nearby countryside. She lives in a charming caravan wagon that is pulled by an old hare named Hasa. In her wagon, she carries all sorts of wondrous things: spices, herbs, teas, medicines and magic. She also carries many treasures she found in the world beyond Limindoor, some things clearly made by Tall Ones.

Mother Comfrey is nice and round. She dresses in soft green velvet and tucks her gray hair under a little white lacy cap on top of which sits her formidable lavender colored gnome's hat.

As noted before, she is always the Mistress of Ceremonies at the Gnomes' Thanks-Giving Celebration. That is a fitting thing as of all the gnomes in and around Limindoor she is perhaps the one gnome that everyone, animals included, is most *grateful* for.

When Mother Comfrey stepped from her wagon, quite spryly for a gnome who was *several* hundred years of age, her first thought was to care for Hasa. It is because of Hasa that she was able to move around the countryside with such ease and tend to those in need.

Over the years, Mother Comfrey has had many other hares pull her wagon, you may be sure. But for now, the hare she relies on is Hasa. Such is the 'Cycle of Life.'

"Come, Friends, let us gather around," she called out to the group.

Everyone circled the fire pit with hands, paws and such all joined together as was possible so they might all share in saying the opening verse:

> *"Earth who gives to us this food,*
> *Sun, who makes it ripe and good,*
> *Sun above, Earth below,*
> *Our loving thanks to you we show.*

We thank you for the blossoms,
And for nuts and fruit,
We thank you for the stems and leaves,
We thank you for the roots!"

- A traditional gnome blessing

"How wonderful it is for us to be all together again for our Thanks-Giving Celebration!" she said.

"Let us first welcome those who have not celebrated this event with us before. I see we have Meggy and Gus here. Welcome, you two. And to all of you baby birds, squirrel youngsters, and oh so many new rabbits as well, let's say welcome! "

"Welcome! Welcome! We are glad you are here!" called out the crowd.

"And to our dear, dear friend who is no longer with us, Mees," added Mother Comfrey. "Let us all show our gratitude for his friendship!"

The crowd stood for a moment in silence, in respect for their friend. Then, in one voice they all called out, "Thank you! Thank you, Mees, for being our good friend!"

Those who were holding hands and paws then passed a friendly squeeze around the circle. (Have you ever done that, Reader? It's such a fun way to share in being a part of a group.)

"So, now my friends," continued Mother Comfrey, "let the festival begin!"

All at once, there was a scurry to get things ready.

Mossy was down on his knees with his flint and tinder lighting the bonfire. In no time at all bright flames were dancing about.

"Now, why don't we get that acorn-bucket line started so we can fill our pot here with that good Muddy Brook water?" asked Mother Comfrey holding up the treasured Gratitude Soup Pot for all to see. Clearly, she had recently polished it, for it shone brightly in the light of the growing flames.

"Then we can get our soup started with all of those food treasures you brought to share!"

When the pot was filled with fresh water, each gnome dropped in their contribution of vegetables, mushrooms, and herbs. Even Meggy added a dollop of golden butter she had brought from home. (Making butter was one of her favorite chores at home.)

When the delicious scent of the soup filled the Commons, everyone's mouth started watering. It would be a while before it was ready though.

People stood and sat. They munched and milled about, both at the table and close to the fire, chatting amongst themselves as if they hadn't seen each other in ages.

At last Mother Comfrey called them together. "Let us have our story now, while our soup is cooking," she said.

So everyone took their places again. Sitting together there they were warmed by the fire and by the friendship of being with their companions.

6.
A Story

The gnomes settled into the cushion of crisp autumn leaves and watched as glowing sparks from the fire flew up towards the sky.

Each of the various animals in attendance had also found their place so that they too might hear the story.

Mother Comfrey sat into a great moss-covered log chair that had been rolled out from somewhere and readied for her.

"My friends, I am going to tell you the story about how we gnomes came to value Generosity so much," she began at last.

"Many, many generations ago, long before the Wise Ones had taught us 'The Way', there lived a gnome from the Stone family.

Rumor has it that he was one of the *first* of the Stone gnomes!"

When the group around the circle heard that, they cheered for Pebble. And those next to him patted him on the back.

Gus and Meggy were puzzled by that until Mother Comfrey explained that Pebble, *their* Pebble, was a descendant of that very same Stone family.

"Yes, my friends," Mother Comfrey continued, "in fact, Pebble here was named after the gnome in the story… the first of many. Of course, this *first* Pebble became known as 'Sir Pebble' since his story was to go down in our gnome history.

"Well, on one particular day, this *first* Pebble, who was already quite old, was out taking a walk. As he walked along the path, minding his own business, thinking about whatever gnomes thought about in those days…he kicked up a stone.

"Now, who here hasn't had that happen to them?" she asked looking around the fire. "You are walking along, not paying attention to where you are walking, and, *thud!* Your foot kicks a stone!"

To that, there was much nodding in agreement by the gnomes.

"But, something about that *particular* stone caught Pebble's eye. So he picked it up and rubbed the dust off of it with his thumb.

"And he saw the most amazing thing! The stone *sparkled* with shimmering flashes of rainbow-colored light.

"Pebble stood there amazed at the stone's glittering colors.

After a while he put the stone into his bag - only to remove it, again and again, to gaze at its splendor. He just could *not resist* looking at it, as it was so very beautiful.

"Now, I bet you are all thinking that Pebble being a *good Gentle-gnome*, didn't keep that stone for long. *Surely* he must have given it to someone else right away.

"But no. *He did keep it.* Remember, my friends, this was *before* gnomes knew anything of 'The Way of Kindness and Generosity.'

"Not that Pebble was a *stingy gnome*; no not at all. He just felt since he had been so lucky to *find* that amazing stone, that it was *his* and he would just *keep it*. And that is what he did.

"Now, my friends, I know that many of us old gnomes have many aches and pains in our old bones - mostly when it is damp or cold. Well, that First Pebble had those aches and pains too.

"But after he found that stone, a wondrous thing started to happen. *His aches and pains disappeared.* And Pebble started to feel so much *energy* that he could easily dash up any hill, and run along any path - just as he had done when he was a *youngster*."

"Well, those of you who have heard this story know that this change was because the stone was a *magic healing stone.*

"But Pebble didn't know that!

"Now my friends, I want you to think about something for a moment. Are you all listening?

"When you feel really, *really good* don't you feel something *magical* happen inside you? Don't you feel like your heart just fills up with *kindness and generosity*?

"Well, that is what happened to Pebble. As soon as he started feeling *really good*, his heart was so filled up with *kindness* that he just couldn't wait to do nice things for *everyone!*

"In fact, the first kind thing he thought to do was to *give away* that beautiful stone - which, of course, is what he did.

"Now," said Mother Comfrey, "just imagine how surprised some lucky gnome must have been, so long ago, when Pebble went up to him and handed him that remarkable stone, and for no apparent reason? Gnomes just *didn't do* that kind of thing in those days.

"Well, we all know that the other gnome accepted the stone. And, in no time the stone worked its magic on him as well, just as it had done to Pebble.

"So, as soon as *that* gnome started feeling *kind and generous,* what do you think he did?

"Yes, he passed the stone on to *another* gnome!

"Soon, *everyone* in that village had owned the stone for a while *and* had experienced its magic. For each gnome was not only *cured* of their aches and pains, but their hearts *became filled* with kindness and generosity as well."

When they heard that, everyone sitting around the fire chuckled and nodded to each other.

"However, *oddly,*" continued Mother Comfrey, "no one thought that the way they felt was because of the *stone itself.* They thought it was because they had *given the stone away.*

"They thought that it was *the act of giving* that made them feel so good!

"After a while," she explained further, "the gnomes forgot all about that stone and *became kind and generous all the time.*"

"What happened to the stone, Mother Comfrey? Was it lost?" asked Gus. He was fascinated by all of this, never having heard this story before.

"No my boy; it was not lost. *I* had it!" she replied.

"You?" he gasped.

"When one of the gnomes gave it to me," she explained, "I *sensed* it had *healing* powers. Before long though I realized it had *magical* powers as well.

It was, in fact, a *magic healing-stone.* For it had healed the gnomes' hearts as well as all of their ills and pains!"

"Do you still have it, Mother Comfrey? Can we see it, please?" blurted Meggy.

Her eyes were shining at the thought of seeing something so beautiful - for she was sure it must be a *Fairy Stone*.

"No, no, my Dear, I do not still have it. But what happened with the stone is another story - for another time.

"You see, all the while the stone was there in the village it had done a *Very Important Thing*. It had started the 'Cycle of Kindness and Generosity' that we *now all live by*.

"And it wasn't long before that Cycle spread throughout *the entire World of Gnome*.

'So *that*, my friends, is why, when we meet another gnome, we are always generous. Because it just 'feels' so good to give to others"

The group sat there in silence. They gazed into the fire and thought about her story. They reflected on how right she was.

It did feel so very good to be generous!

7.
Gratitude

Mother Comfrey stood up to give the simmering soup a stir. "Mmm, this soup smells like it's ready. Who would like some?"

Brother Acorn passed his basket of cups and bowls around for people to choose from. Then, one by one each stepped forward to get their serving of soup.

Now, Dear Reader is the time for you to learn something about gnomes that you surely did not know before. Gnomes are very fond of punning! (A pun is a joke made by using two words that sound the same but have a different meaning.)

Since there are some folks out there who really cannot abide puns, you are hereby 'warned' that gnomes just *love* puns!

As everyone sat down and slurped their soup, as tidily as possible, one of the gnomes called across the fire.

"Okay, who knows when the moon is the heaviest?"

To which someone said, "Gosh, I give up. When?"

Then the gnome who had first asked the question, replied with a chuckle, "When it's *full!*"

After their laughter quieted down someone else asked, "Did you know that for a toadstool to grow you have to give it as *mushroom* as possible?"

At that, one of the gnomes, we won't say who laughed so hard he *spilled* his soup.

"Okay, tell me, what bow can't be tied?"

"Oh, oh, I know that, is it a 'rainbow?'"

"Ha, ha," they replied with glee. "A rain*bow*!!"

"Well, my friends, last night I tried to catch some fog," said one. After a pause, he added, "I *mist!*"

Can you imagine the silliness? So many snorts and giggles.

"Aren't you all a nutty lot," said Mother Comfrey to them kindly. When they heard that they all laughed again and toasted her by holding up their acorn *nut* cups and wal*nut* shell bowls.

"Well, it sure didn't take us long to finish off this good soup, my friends. Look how clean the pot is," she said picking it up to inspect it.

Yes, every drop of that delicious Gratitude Soup was gone. The soup that had been made with contributions from each gnome had been enjoyed by all with great gusto.

Mother Comfrey peered into the pot and said, "Now that the soup is all gone, I have a surprise for you."

She signaled to Meggy who scooped another dollop of butter into the pot. (Clearly, they had planned this in advance). Everyone looked questioningly at each other…. What was going to happen?

Then, from the basket she always carried with her, Mother Comfrey withdrew a small cloth bag. From the bag, she took a number of what appeared to be polished brass pebbles. These she threw, one-by-one, into the pot. Then she sat back and looked around the circle with twinkling eyes and a mischievous grin.

A perplexed silence fell on the group. "Whatever was she doing?" they wondered.

Suddenly, there was a very loud POP!!!! And everyone jumped!

Like magic, a strange, white, puffy object had flown up out of the pot and landed right on Gilly's lap. It was about the size of a large apple and was warm and smelled *very* good. Whatever *was* that thing they wondered? (Reader, can you guess?)

A moment later there was another loud POP!!!! And another puffy thing leaped out - this time into Wren's lap. Then another one bumped Brother Acorn's shoulder and one fell at Pebble's feet. POP! POP! POP! High up they flew, then down again. One even knocked Mossy's tall cap right off of his head!

At first, Meggy and Gus were as puzzled as the others. Then they laughed out loud when they realized what that large puffy thing was that had just dropped to the ground between them.

Do you know what it was yet, Reader? If you thought it was *popcorn*, you were right!

"Go on - you can eat it. You will find it's quite yummy," Mother Comfrey said as she dropped a few more 'pebbles' into the pot.

The gnomes tentatively held their puffs to their mouths and nibbled. Never in their very long lives had the gnomes ever tasted anything like *that* before!

Reader, if you were wondering whether or not Gilly grew corn in his garden – he did not. After all, how could he have ever harvested something that tall? It was because he didn't, that the gnomes had never encountered such a thing as corn before – not in their very long lives.

Gus and Meggy realized that Mother Comfrey had once again brought another 'Wonder' from the Tall Ones' world to share with the gnomes of Limindoor Woods. She was always full of surprises.

8.
Thanks

As each of the gnomes finished their popcorn puff and politely licked their fingers clean, Wren picked up her flute and started to play the music for the Gratitude Song. (That music can be found at the back of this book on page 224.)

One-by-one, the others joined in by humming. Then Mother Comfrey's clear and strong voice started the song;

♪ "I give thanks, I give thanks, for the healing herbs. Summer is gone, autumn is here. Soon it will be cold." ♪

All the gnomes knew that Mother Comfrey worked much of her magic, healing their ills, by using the treasure of various herbs that grew in and around Limindoor. So that is why she chose to thank the herbs.

The gnomes then joined in, singing the reply, echoing what she had sung:

♪ "We give thanks, we give thanks, for the healing herbs. Summer is gone, autumn is here. Soon it will be cold." ♪

In turn, each gnome around the circle, sang a verse of the song, adding the *one main thing* that they were grateful for. Even Gus and Meggy decided to join in. (Reader, if you like, you can read what each one said at the end of the book on page 225.)

After they had all sung their thanks, Wren took out her wooden flute and played the music to the song once again. Everyone hummed along and thought of all the other things that they hadn't mentioned that they were grateful for.

And then all became silent.

When a single twig made a final loud snap in the dimming fire it was as if it had signaled the end of the festival.

There they all sat in the quiet of the fading light, silently reflecting on all that had happened that night.

They thought of the good food, the music, the story, and the singing. They thought of Mother Comfrey's white puff surprises. And of all the gratitude they felt.

What a very happy place Limindoor Woods was to live in.

9.
Rosette

As the night drew near, several stars blinked into view overhead. Although the festival had ended, the gnomes and animals still sat around the fire and gazed - transfixed by the dimming flicker of its fading embers.

"Ahem! Excuse me!" said a tiny voice. "Hello? I do hope I am not bothering you…"

Everyone was startled as if they had awakened from a dream. Had someone spoken?

"Excuse me. I am looking for Mr. Mossy. Is he - is he here, by any chance?"

Then they saw her - a tiny slip of a mouse. She was barely *half* the size of their dear friend, Mees. And she was so pale! In the fading light of the evening, her fur shone as dimly as a wisp of fog.

Fortunately, Mossy had his wits about him. He stood and approached the tiny creature.

"I am Mossy," he said kindly. "And, to whom am I speaking, My Dear?"

"How do you do Mr. Mossy?" she said with a tiny voice. "My name is Rosette. My mother said that that means 'little rose'."

"Indeed it does," replied Mossy. "What may I do for you, Miss Rosette?"

When the mouse took a step towards Mossy everyone could see that she had a slight limp. But she was so graceful that she somehow managed to make it look as if she was curtsying.

"I have come to stay with you, Mr. Mossy, since my cousin Mees is now gone; if that is alright with you."

A quiet gasp of surprise and delight circled around the group. How fortunate for Mossy who had been so sad of late. Just imagine, now he would have a *new* mouse to keep him company after all; especially with the loneliness of winter ahead.

But, with their joy came a wave of concern about the size of the little girl mouse. For all the gnomes knew how hard Limindoor winters could be, especially on one so small.

The Knitting Gnomes decided, on the spot, that they would have to do something about that *right away*.

"Come to stay with *me*, you say? Oh! Why, yes, Rosette, that is most kind," replied Mossy who was clearly quite overwhelmed. He had not expected someone to come so soon after Mees. Usually, it was months before a new mouse came to stay. And, he too had noticed the mouse's frailness and shared a similar concern about her.

At last Mossy realized that it was up to him to make the next move.

"Well, we are almost finished here, Rosette. We have only just ended our festival and have yet to tidy up. After that I will be happy to show you your new home," he said.

"Is there anything I can do to help?" asked Rosette as if she were already a member of the community.

Wren stepped forward and invited the mouse to accompany her while she cleaned and put away Brother Acorn's treasured acorn cups.

Everyone stepped to it, as always, each doing their share of setting things right.

Mossy oversaw that the embers in the fire were completely doused. After the stones that had circled the fire had cooled sufficiently, they were returned to the stream bed. Gilly and Pebble took the bark table plank back to Gilly's garden.

Several frisky squirrels were glad to help by scattering the pile of leaves all about the

Commons - making an even, soft blanket to cover the earth below.

Mossy busily started lighting the acorn-cap candles. These would light the gnomes' ways home through the growing darkness.

To be honest, even as they were tidying up, many gnomes guardedly glanced over at Rosette. Though they were all quite curious about her they also knew it would not be seemly to pry. There would be time enough to meet her and welcome her to her new home in Limindoor Woods.

10.
A Fright

It was just as some of the gnomes were starting to leave, carrying their little acorn-cap candles, that it happened!

Old Hibou, the owl, who had been sitting on a high branch overlooking the festivities, had just woken up.

Since he'd been coming to the Gnomes' Thanks-Giving Celebration for many years he was pretty sure he had heard *all* of the stories already. So he had fallen asleep. But now, story time was clearly over and people were up and about and gathering their things to leave.

"Oh, ho, ho! What was *that*?"

Something very small and very pale was moving right below him among the fallen leaves. Was that a *mouse???*

In one silent waft, the owl swooped down. His eyes were as round as two bright moons, his claws outstretched wide, like the branches of a tree. Down he flew to the grass, landing right in front of the wisp of pale fur that had caught his attention.

Rosette (for surely you know it was she whom he had spied), firmly stood her ground as she looked up at the enormous bird that towered menacingly over her.

Just at that moment both Wren and Pebble noticed what was happening. Their mouths went dry. No one had thought to warn Old Hibou about the newcomer.

This could be a disaster!

Before they could say anything, though, the pale little mouse had taken an unsteady step *towards* the owl and introduced herself. (Yes, it was true, that step did resemble a curtsy.)

"Good evening, Sir," Rosette said in her tiny, but clear voice as she looked bravely up into the owl's shining eyes.

"My name is Rosette. I am new to Limindoor. I have come to stay with Mr. Mossy - now that my cousin Mees is gone. My mother *told* me that an *owl* lived here in Limindoor. I - I am pleased to meet you, Sir."

Old Hibou was stunned. It was instinct of course that stirred his first most natural response - which was to pluck the creature off the grass and fly away with it. But, now that she had spoken to him, well, flying off with her wouldn't do. No, it wouldn't do at *all!*

Wren and Pebble were panic-stricken. They were terrified that the owl would forget his manners and take the mouse.

But Old Hibou instead, fluffed his feathers; half closed his eyes and replied to the mouse.

"Ahem," he said. "My name is Mr. Hibou. It is a pleasure to meet you, too. Yes, a pleasure." After a pause, he added, "Ahem, well, good night then. Good night, young lady," he said again and turned away.

Upon seeing the two petrified gnomes standing there Mr. Hibou nodded in their direction and said, "Good night Wren. Goodnight Pebble," Then up he flew - up and off into the dark night sky.

Wren and Pebble gazed at Rosette with admiration.

Mossy had been elsewhere lighting candles but had managed to turn just in time to see the very last of what had happened. In fact, *everyone* who remained in the Commons had seen.

"My, what courage it must have taken for Rosette to speak to an *owl* in that way," they all thought. There were many Limindoor gnomes who felt a little intimidated by Old Hibou's sternness.

It's true that the owl had 'befriended' Wren, who was his neighbor. And there were many a night he had accompanied Pebble by flying around the gnome as he climbed Star Mountain to gather Star Seeds. But Old Hibou could also be a little scary!

"Is the tidying up all done?" asked Rosette blithely as she looked around at the gnomes standing there.

"Yes, Rosette, it looks like we are finished here. I think it's time for us *all* to go home," said Wren, still very impressed by the courage that little wisp of a creature had shown.

It was only then that Mother Comfrey stepped out of the shadows and approached Rosette. Though she had been off tending to her hare Hasa, she had returned just in time to observe the owl and mouse encounter. There was something she wished to say to Rosette.

By that time there were only a few gnomes left in the Commons. So only a few actually saw the very touching scene of their dear, round Mother Comfrey lean over the very tiny mouse, say something to her, and then gently kiss her on the nose.

No one had the slightest idea what she had said. Though gnomes do not tend to be nosey, you can be certain that everyone there, having seen what had happened, would wonder about it later - wonder "What *was* it that Mother Comfrey had said to the little mouse."

After Rosette finally said goodbye to Mother Comfrey, she scurried as best as she could (with her limp) back to Mossy's side. She looked up at him and said, "Can we go to your home now, Mr. Mossy? I am really tired."

Soon the Commons was empty.

The wonderful Gnomes' Thanks-Giving Celebration was finally over.

11.
A New Home

The festival had ended and everyone made their way home again holding out their little winking acorn-cup candles to light the way.

Teasel and Tweed had accompanied Meggy back to her portal at the forest edge. The moon shone down on her and lit the way as she crossed through the meadow towards home.

Gus had decided to walk back with Pebble, instead of with Mossy. He had sensed that his Gnome-papa would probably want the time to get to know little Rosette better.

(Reader, don't you think that was a very 'grown-up' choice for Gus to make? Surely, he *must* have been just as curious as the others were about that little mouse.)

Mossy first accompanied Brother Acorn to his home, with young Rosette trailing close behind. Mindful of his old friend, he wanted to be sure that he got home safely in the dark. Then he and the little mouse turned back to make their way silently to Mossy's front porch.

"I am very pleased that you have come, Little Rosette. I hope that you will be happy here," Mossy finally said as he opened his door.

Mossy was still mourning the loss of his friend. Even though he knew more than most about the 'Cycle of Life', he still felt sadness in his heart. There were times he'd often forget and say something to Mees – only to remember that his mouse friend was no longer there with him.

And, as to Rosette coming - well, of course, he had known from past experience that another mouse relative from Mees's family would eventually join him. Mees himself had come to live with him in that way.

It had been just about seven years before, soon after Mossy had just lost *another* dear companion-mouse that a *very young* Mees had come to Mossy's door. Such had been the way of things for him since Mus, his first mouse friend.

Mossy quickly arranged an old blanket on the floor for Rosette to sleep on. "This is where your cousin used to sleep. Will this be alright for you?"

"Oh, yes, Mr. Mossy. It is lovely. I have never slept *inside a tree* before. You know that I live, I mean, I lived, with my brothers and sisters under Stone Wall. That's between Apple Tree Hill and Muddy Brook. Sometimes it's damp there. But *this* is very cozy. Thank you."

"Well, tomorrow, I will show you around Limindoor, if you like. Goodnight, Little Rosette."

Mossy snuffed out the beeswax candle and the room became dark but for a soft glow of moonlight that shone through the window. Soon Rosette heard the gentle rumble of the gnome's snore.

But Little Rosette could not settle down. She kept on squirming and wriggling around on the blanket. She was so used to sleeping with her large jumble of a family that, for her, that solitary place on the floor was far too lonely. So, without even thinking about it, she tried to climb up on Mossy's bed.

Again and again, she tried to jump up but just could not quite make it. Eventually, her scratching and scrambling roused Mossy. Without a word, the sleepy old gnome picked the slim creature up, settled her at the foot of his bed and curled the old blanket about her like a nest.

From then on, as long as Rosette lived in Limindoor that was where she would always sleep.

At the break of the new day, Mossy lay for a while in his warm bed. As always, he took that time to think of the many things he was grateful for.

Always, at the top of his list was his friendship with Mees. But that thought started to make him sad when he realized how *alone* he was now that Mees was gone.

Suddenly, Mossy recalled that he was *not alone* anymore.

First, he looked at the place on the floor where he had put the little newcomer, but no one was there.

Then remembering the night before, he looked down, over his beard, to the foot of the bed. There he saw a little wisp of a pale tail peeking out from under Mees's old blanket.

It was Little Rosette's tail!

12.
New Friends

It was a new day. And Mossy had a new companion.

The two of them had risen with the dawn. Mossy had made his bed, combed his beard and was finishing up his cup of dewdrop tea. Rosette was daintily munching on the last crumbs of a very tasty seed cake.

Mossy realized that in the dim light of the previous evening he hadn't been able to get a proper look at the little mouse. So, as politely as he could, he glanced down at her.

What a curious little creature she was. She was so much smaller than Mees had been that she could scarcely reach to the top of the table. "It's no surprise she couldn't climb up on the bed," Mossy thought to himself.

Her black eyes, though, were *enormous*. They were bright and very quick as she looked here and there taking in every detail of her new home.

And those ears! No wonder her name meant "little rose." Her ears were as pink and petite and round as tiny rose petals.

In the daylight, he saw that her fur also seemed to have a light pinkish tint. But on closer inspection, he saw it was because her hair was so pale it was almost transparent, and the pink of her skin shone through. Rosette, indeed!

Then he remembered that he'd seen a slight limp when she walked. Again, making sure that she wasn't looking (he did not wish to embarrass her) he quickly peeked down at her legs. Yes, he could see that her left hind foot was indeed lame. He hoped it did not cause her pain. He also hoped she'd be willing to talk about it someday. But for now, he knew that it would be neither appropriate nor kind to ask her about it outright.

"Would you like to take a tour around Limindoor, Rosette? Or would you prefer to rest here?" asked Mossy before realizing that maybe a walk wouldn't be such a good idea for her after all.

"Oh, yes! I mean, no! Oh, Mossy, I want to see *everything!*" she stated very emphatically.

"Well then, off we go, if you are ready," he said slinging his bag over his back and opening the door.

As Mossy stepped outside he almost trod on a lovely crystal that was sitting on his front step. "What's this?" he asked.

"Ah, ha!" he exclaimed. "I bet this was meant for you, Rosette. I'll bet that good old Pebble, our neighbor, must have stopped by early this morning after his work in the crystal cave. He works all night you see, taking care of planting and polishing the crystals.

"Ooh, how pretty it is," said the mouse inspecting it. "I've never been given a gift before. Can we keep it out here in the sun where it's so sparkly?"

"Whatever you like, Rosette," he said smiling. Then he thought to himself, "I have certainly never met a mouse like you before, Little One."

The first gnome they visited was Brother Acorn. (Reader, if you check the Limindoor map on page 11 you can follow the route they took that day.)

On the way there Mossy found a lovely pinecone to give to his friend. And when they arrived, he handed it to him and said, "Good morning Brother Acorn. I thought we'd take a walk so Rosette could see Limindoor Woods in the daytime. We came to see you first."

"Well, a very good morning to you both. And thank you, Mossy for this lovely pinecone. Oh, look, it's still filled with many delicious pine-nuts!"

Brother Acorn quickly stepped back into his house to get something. "And this is for you, young lady," he said as he held out a very tiny, polished acorn-cap bowl for Rosette to drink out of.

Rosette, unaccustomed to receiving gifts, looked first at the bowl and then at Brother Acorn with an amazed look on her face.

"Oh, dear," thought Mossy realizing that Rosette had still much to learn. "Rosette, when someone gives you something you say 'thank you'," he explained.

"Now, won't this be a nice bowl for you to drink your tea from, dear?" he said as he put the bowl in his bag.

"Th-thank you, Brother Acorn," stated the mouse as she gazed up at the old gnome.

"That's right, Rosette. Well said.

"Our Brother Acorn here is the Guardian of the Trees. He planted most of the oaks and many other trees that grow in Limindoor, as well," said Mossy gesturing around to the forest. "Maybe someday you would like to join him when he goes planting."

Rosette nodded and smiled eagerly at that.

"Well, we have a distance to go today, my friend," he said to Brother Acorn. "I imagine you want to rest up after last night's celebration, so we will say goodbye for now."

As they walked off, Rosette stopped and turned. Looking back she saw that Brother Acorn was still standing in his doorway - so she raised her tiny paw and waved at him. As they walked on, she said to Mossy, "He's very nice."

Mossy just smiled.

The next gnome they visited was Gilly. Mossy explained to Rosette that Gilly was a gardening gnome. That it was his constant, hard and loving work in his garden that provided *all* the gnomes in Limindoor with good fresh food to eat.

When they arrived, Gilly gave Rosette the very last strawberry of the season as a welcoming gift and Rosette remembered to say 'thank you' right away. She was enjoying this 'giving' business very much. The gnomes of Limindoor Woods were all so friendly.

13.
More Gifts

Wren was the next gnome they went to visit. She lived just north of the Commons, up off the ground in what had been a vacant squirrels' home in an aged oak tree.

(In case you are wondering how a gnome could live so high off the ground, you should know that some kind gnomes had built her a sturdy staircase that curved up around the trunk of the tree, right to her doorway.)

Rosette was disappointed when they arrived at Wren's home-tree and found that she wasn't there. The mouse had so wanted to talk to Wren about her flute playing.

For, you see, the night before during the festival, Rosette had actually been standing off to the side for *quite a while* and had witnessed much of the Gnomes' Thanks-Giving Celebration. It was only after some time that she'd decided to come forward and ask for Mossy.

When she'd heard Wren's flute playing she was so impressed she just couldn't wait to hear more of it.

As Mossy and Rosette walked on, Mossy silently pointed out where Old Hibou, Wren's *owl* neighbor, was asleep on a high branch of a nearby tree. Rosette nodded with understanding.

"Wren often likes to spend time here in the Commons playing her music, Rosette," explained Mossy as they entered the small meadow. "This is where last night's festival was held. Do you recognize it?"

Rosette shook her head. Nothing looked familiar. And she couldn't see any evidence of the night's merrymaking - for the tidying up had been complete.

Their next stop was Teasel and Tweed's home. Those two Knitting Gnomes must have, either stayed up late working through the night or had awakened very early that morning. For when they opened their door the first thing they did was present Rosette with a lovely, soft, pink, mouse-sized blanket they had just finished knitting!

"We hope you have many cozy nights with this, Rosette," Teasel said.

And Tweed added, "We know how cold these winter nights can be. And we were pretty sure that by now Mees's old blanket must have become quite threadbare."

"That is very true," admitted Mossy. "Isn't this a thoughtful gift, Rosette?"

Rosette buried her pink nose into the fluffy softness of the wool. To be honest, she was so moved by the gift that she couldn't even manage to say 'thank you' to the gnomes.

"There, there, Little One, you just take it home and enjoy it. We hope it brings you many sweet mousey dreams," said the brothers.

At the mention of sleep, Rosette could barely suppress a yawn. She was feeling very much in the need of a nap. So after their goodbyes, Mossy and the mouse headed home again, laden with her gifts.

When they returned home who should they find sitting in their yard waiting for them, but Meggy and Gus?

The children, each on their own, had reacted to Rosette's arrival with mixed feelings. They were certainly excited that Mossy would have a new companion. And they were curious about who the little creature was. Yet, like everyone else, they were also concerned about how fragile she looked.

When Meggy returned home after the celebration, she immediately went to her toy chest to look through her doll's clothes. Meggy, an able knitter, had made several fine garments for Emily, her doll. When she asked Emily if she'd be willing to give up a lovely soft sage-green sweater she had knitted for her, Emily did not reply. So Meggy took the doll's silence as a "yes."

Meggy counted on the sweater becoming smaller when she brought it through the magic portal and hoped it would be just the right size for the mouse.

(Reader, in case you didn't know – *almost anything* the children carried with them when *entering* through the magic portal into Limindoor Woods became *small*, just like they did. And, conversely, *almost* anything they carried *out* with them when they left Limindoor would grow large again. You will hear later about what didn't change size.)

That day, the two children, thinking that Mossy probably would still want time to get to know his new mouse friend, decided to keep their visit very brief. And after that, they planned on taking a walk so that they might further explore Limindoor Woods.

Remember, Reader, that as small as Limindoor Woods might look on the map, once you became gnome-sized, as they had, the whole area of the woods became proportionally *much, much larger*. Believe it or not, there were still many parts of Limindoor the children had yet to explore.

So, there were the children patiently sitting in Mossy's yard when Mossy and Rosette returned home.

Meggy could hardly wait to present the tiny wooly sweater to Rosette and was so happy when it turned out to be a perfect fit.

It's true, none of the animals, either in or out of Limindoor, ever wore 'people clothes.' That would be silly, wouldn't it? But, somehow, it just seemed right that Little Rosette, with her thin silky fur, would welcome a little warmth in the coming cold days of winter. And the soft green of the wool looked so lovely with her light pink coloring.

Gus had brought popovers. His mother, famed for her baking, delighted in making bunches of them for him whenever he went into the woods. Gus had really hoped to give the mouse something more personal but couldn't think of what it should be.

Rosette proudly showed the children the other gifts she had received that morning.

When the children asked her about her first night there, Rosette told them how much she liked living inside a tree. But she admitted to having been lonely sleeping on the floor. She said since she was so used to sleeping with her very large wiggly family that she had wanted to climb up to be with Mossy.

She said her scrambling to climb up on the bed had unfortunately wakened him up. And only after he had lifted her up onto the bed had she been finally able to go to sleep at his feet.

That gave Gus an idea!

"Mossy," he said excitedly. "May I quickly make something for Rosette, so that her climb will be easier?"

"Certainly Gus, go ahead. I would welcome being able to sleep the night through," he chuckled. "And I am sure that Rosette here would be happy to come and go as she pleased. Wouldn't you, my dear?" he said smiling down at the mouse.

"I would. Yes, I would, Mossy" she replied very seriously.

"What are you going to make, Gus?" asked Meggy.

"You'll see," he said with a grin. First, he measured how high the bed was and then promising to be right back, he stepped outdoors in search of just the right piece of bark.

He found one right away and with his special whittling knife, (which he always carried in his bag) he carved a hole in one end of the plank of bark. Then he fit a short stick into the hole, like a peg.

Once inside Mossy's home again, Gus securely propped the plank against the foot of the bed, making a sort of rough ramp for Rosette to climb on. When he asked her to try it out she almost trembled with joy… overwhelmed by such generosity.

"Well, Gus, it looks like you have certainly taken care of that problem," admired Mossy. "What do you have to say to him, Rosette?"

"Oh, thank you. Thank you both for your gifts!" said the little mouse as she scurried up and down her very own ramp a couple of times… of course still wearing her fancy new sweater.

When the children said their goodbyes and left to take their walk, Mossy went out to have a quiet sit-down on his bench.

He lit his Bearberry pipe and stared into the forest, deep in thought. Yes, my friend, you may be sure that his thoughts soon turned to his absent friend, Mees.

Rosette so tired from her very busy morning, once again happily climbed up her new little ramp. Then, wearing her new sweater, she curled up with her brand new blanket at the foot of the bed and took a restful nap.

14.
The Explorers

The two children having just left Mossy's, stepped onto the main woodland path heading north.

Meggy was the first to speak. "Gus, what do you think of Rosette?" she asked.

"I think she is very nice," he said at once. A moment later he added, "But she sure is tiny, compared to Mees, that is."

"Well, she may be tiny, but I think she has a lot of *pluck*!" she countered.

"What is pluck, Meggy?"

"You know. It means 'courage' or 'grit.' That's what my Pop calls it. Remember how she faced Mr. Hibou last night? She was *fearless*. Why even I was scared of him. And she walked *right up* to him. Yup, she has 'pluck!'" stated Meggy.

"Well, I am glad my Gnome-papa isn't going to be lonely anymore," Gus added.

After they walked a bit further, Gus asked, "Say, Meggy, you know, last night at the festival, when they got the water for the soup from the creek?"

"Mmm?"

"Well, I was thinking about that, and I realized I've *never* checked out that part of the woods before. Muddy Brook is the same stream that runs through my back yard, but I never followed up to this side of Limindoor. I thought it would be fun to explore.

"But, I was also wondering... I mean, I've never left Limindoor through *any other way* than our portals before."

"Gosh, Gus, do you think the same magic will happen on this side of the woods?"

"I don't know. But I guess we can find out. Do you want to go with me, Meggy?"

"Okay. I guess. Sure. If Rosette is 'plucky' then so am I!" stated Meggy as if convincing herself.

The children had just passed the turn-off to Gilly's garden and were approaching the entrance to the Commons and the tree with the famous Ding-Dong on it.

"Meggy, what does the Ding-Dong look like to you? You know if it were a *lot smaller…*"

Meggy looked up at the strange metal device and admitted, "I don't know. Maybe it's a key?"

"Yes! I think so too. It *is* a key! I am sure of it. I told Mossy I thought it might have something to do with that old door that Pebble showed me – you know, the one I told you about, that's high up on the side of Star Mountain."

"What did Mossy say then?"

"He told me that since the thing had been buried in the ground a long time there was no need to rush to find out. He said I should be more patient.

Actually, it was Mees who seemed more interested in the whole thing. He even suggested that I talk it over with *Pebble* since it was Pebble who had shown me the door."

"And did you ask him?" queried Meggy.

"No, but I still think about it a lot."

"Look, Meggy," said Gus as they approached a high, graceful canopy of ferns to the west side of the Commons. "Isn't this the direction they went to get the water?"

When the two children peered from under a gigantic fern frond they were amazed.

They saw that they were standing on a pebbly shore and, sweeping only a short distance in front of them was a *vast deep river*. It's slow, powerful current flowed around a number of boulders that were strewn across the waterway.

Beyond the river, the children could see a very high grass covered hill with the suggestion of a dark tree line far off in the distance.

The children just stared at it with an astonished look on their faces.

"Wow! This is *Muddy Brook*?" asked Gus, truly surprised to see how greatly the stream had grown in size.

"Come on, Meggy," said Gus as he took her hand and they bravely stepped down onto the riverbank. Suddenly, both of them slipped on the gravel. After catching their footing they looked up and were even *more astonished* with what they saw.

The immense river they had seen just a moment before had suddenly shrunk into a small gurgling brook. The massive boulders had transformed into handy stepping stones – stones they might use to easily cross the stream.

"What???" the two said in unison. And then they laughed. Ah ha! They had gotten *through* the portal! And they were *full* sized Tall Ones again!

The children turned back to look where had just exited and saw a mass of rich green ferns - now barely higher than their knees.

"Well, we better not forget where this is if we want to get back into Limindoor from this side of the woods," said Meggy wisely. When she turned to Gus she started giggling.

"Oh, Gus! Your hat!!! Look at your gnome hat!" she laughed.

Gus, as he had always done, had put on his gnome hat when he entered the woods that morning. But, this was the *first time* he had forgotten to take it off *before* leaving Limindoor.

Unbeknownst to him, the same magic that changed the size of whatever he took, or was wearing, through the portal had, for some reason, had *no effect* on his hat. (By the way, Reader, that lovely gnome hat had been given to him soon after he had first arrived in Limindoor. Naturally, it had been made by the Knitting Gnomes. It was a special gift to honor him.)

No, his gnome hat had *not* changed size. It was still just as small as it had been moments before when they were in the Commons. It was Gus who had become a *full-size child*. The 'hat', now a bit larger than the thumb of a mitten, lay rakishly atop Gus's hair.

"What?" said Gus, reaching up to his head. "Ha! Would you look at this!"

he exclaimed as he examined the curious tiny object. "I wonder why it didn't change size."

As Gus tucked the tiny hat into his carrying bag he noticed that Meggy was busily arranging some stones.

"What are you doing, Meggy?" he asked.

"There, these stones will be a marker for us so we can find our way back into Limindoor," said Meggy brushing off her hands.

"Say, that's a good idea! Now, let's go see what's on the other side."

15.
Muddy Brook

In little more than a 'hop and skip' the two quickly reached the other side of Muddy Brook. There they found that the high green hill they had seen from Limindoor was nothing other than a low, grassy embankment. It gradually rose onto gently rolling meadow – one that stretched out west for some distance.

"Race you, Meggy," said Gus as he took off at a running pace across the grassy meadow.

Meggy ran too - but not to race. She ran with her arms out wide, just delighting in the feeling of the chill air on her cheeks and the freedom of moving through the wide open space.

"I am going to go look at that old tree," Gus called to her.

In the far northwest corner of the field was a venerable old snag of an oak tree. It was missing several limbs and clearly hadn't had any leaves for many years. Numerous dead branches littered the ground around it.

"Do you think that Brother Acorn planted this one too?" asked Meggy as she caught up with Gus.

"I don't know. But I do know it would make him sad to its condition," he replied.

"Maybe it's just really old, Gus. I don't think oaks live forever."

The two children sat on a large fallen branch for a rest. They looked all around them and then back at Limindoor.

"Isn't it amazing, Gus? I mean Limindoor Woods. Just look at it. It looks like any other forest, but we know how special it is," observed Meggy.

"You're right, Meggy. It *is* special."

Gus, feeling a bit hungry, reached into his bag to bring out two remaining popovers. Just as he offered one to Meggy they heard a loud cawing from the top of the old oak.

Then, whoosh, down flew a very impressive shiny black crow – right down to where the children were sitting.

"Caw," he said. "Caw, caw, caw!"

"Well, hello, to you too," Gus said to the crow.

Meggy tore off a piece of her popover and held it out to the bird.

"Would you like some, Mr. Crow?" she offered.

The crow took a hop forward and politely accepted the pastry from Meggy's hand. Then he did a very curious thing. He bowed his large inky-black head as if in 'thanks', and again call out, "Caw, caw!"

"Gus, did you see what the crow did?" asked Meggy. "He behaved just like Master Kruk did. He bowed as if in 'thanks'! Did you see?"

Reader, perhaps you will recall that sometime before, Meggy, when in Limindoor and therefore *much smaller*, had made the acquaintance of a very large, kind old crow named Master Kruk.

"Are you Master Kruk," Gus asked the bird, half in jest.

To which the crow replied, "Caw, caw!" and cocked his head sideways as he looked at the children.

"I wonder!" said Meggy to Gus. Then, turning towards the crow said, "If you are Master Kruk, then we know you and you know us. I am Meggy, and this here is Gus. We met you in Limindoor, that time you hurt your wing."

The crow continued to cock its head and looked first at one child and then the other.

"We were a lot smaller then – the size of our gnome friends."

"Do you understand us, Master Kruk?" asked Gus. "If you do, please show us, somehow."

With that, the crow swiftly leaped into the air and took flight. He quickly rose to a perch, high atop a broken limb of the oak tree, disappeared behind it a moment and then swooped back down to the children. In his beak was a shiny mother-of-pearl button which he laid at Meggy's feet.

"Oh, my! So you are Master Kruk! Why, thank you, Sir!" said the astonished Meggy. "This is a lovely button!"

"Caw, caw-caw!" replied the crow to Meggy. Then he turned to Gus and said, "Caw-caw-caw! Caw! Caw! Caw!"

"Mr. Kruk, I am sorry, but I cannot understand you. I think it's because we are big again," said Gus with frustration.

At that, the crow, once again, flew up to his cache high in the tree. When he returned to the children he held two metal building-nails in his beak. Those he placed in front of Gus and stated very emphatically, "Caw-caw-caw! Caw! Caw! Caw!"

"Um, thank you, Master Kruk. These are nice nails," said Gus picking them up and examining them. Then, turning to

Meggy he said, "What do you think he is trying to tell me?"

"Gosh, I don't know, Gus." Meggy shrugged.

"But I do know that I need to be getting back soon," she added after a moment. "Why don't we come back here next weekend? Okay?"

They said goodbyes to the crow and started back across the field.

But the crow followed them. "Caw-caw-caw! Caw! Caw! Caw!" he said called, again and again, as he flew up and down in front of them.

"Master Kruk, we're sorry, but we really *can't* understand you! We'll return and see you next week, though," said Gus.

The crow landed in front of them and bowed his head as if in reply to what Gus had said. Then he flew away.

"Well, that was certainly strange," admitted Meggy. "I do wonder what he was trying to tell us."

Soon the children were back at the creek where they quickly spied the stones Meggy had stacked there. They easily crossed the water, without getting a bit wet, and stood before the low ferns.

"What do we do now?" asked Meggy.

"I don't know. I guess we just try to get under those ferns."

Gus reached for Meggy's hand. As they stepped towards the ferns their feet slipped on the gravel again and the children almost fell. When they looked up they saw that the magic had happened once more. They were small again and the opening through the ferns was now a high wide arch that they could easily step under.

As soon as they realized that they were back in Limindoor, Gus dug into his bag and found his gnome hat. Glad to see that it was once again its proper size, he put it on.

"Well, that was fun," he said. "Do you want me to walk you to your portal, Meggy?" (Wasn't that a 'Gentle-gnome-ly' thing to do, Reader – to ask to escort her back?)

"Oh, no thank you, Gus. I think I'll stop by the Knitting Gnomes first. I want to give them this button as a gift. I think they will like it," she said taking it out of her pocket.

(Now, Reader, can you guess what size the button was? Do you think it was the size of a button, like the one on your shirt? Or was it the size of a plate? Pretty confusing, isn't it? Well, just so you know, it *had* shrunk along with the children, to the size of a gnome's button.)

They said their goodbyes and promised to meet the next day on the path near Apple Tree Hill, so they could to go to school together.

Gus made his way down the path towards home.

16.
A Song

The next day all of the gnomes in Limindoor were busy with gnome business. There was not a single 'lazy-gnome' among them as they always loved whatever they were doing – be it gnome work or gnome play!

On that day Little Rosette decided to adventure out from her new home – all by herself.

First, she visited Brother Acorn, but he was entertaining a family of rather noisy squirrels so she decided to come back another time. Then she found her way to Gilly's garden where she met a very friendly rabbit who told her that Gilly was out and about gathering firewood for the winter.

So Rosette continued north on the path and found herself, once again, in the Commons.

Can you imagine her delight when she found Wren sitting on a stump, practicing her flute?

"Well, hello Rosette," said Wren when she opened her eyes and saw the little mouse sitting in front of her. "How nice to see you again!"

"Oh, Wren, your music is *so* beautiful," Rosette sighed. "Please play some more. Would you mind playing what you played at the festival; the song about 'giving thanks'?"

Wren wasn't aware that Rosette had heard her playing at the festival. But she smiled, lifted her flute and began the sweet, simple tune. Rosette sat there and listened – transfixed.

"Oh, that was so lovely," said the mouse when Wren finished her tune. "Thank you so much."

She continued sitting and listening as Wren played other pieces until suddenly Rosette surprised herself by yawning!

"Oh, I'm sorry, Wren," the embarrassed mouse said. "I really *do* like your music. I guess it must be my nap time," she said, getting up to go.

"Oh, that's okay, Rosette. You are welcome here anytime."

As she turned south heading towards Mossy's, Rosette discovered a corner of the Commons she'd not seen before. It was a quiet hidden place among a golden 'forest' of tall, dry grasses. There the gentle autumn sun warmed the earth and brought out the wonderful scent of the meadow's herbs. Rosette decided to stretch out on a patch of dried moss there and quickly fell asleep.

When she awoke, she looked around her and smiled. She decided that she had found her favorite place in *all* of Limindoor Woods - her 'Very Special Place'.

Do you have a 'Very Special Place' Reader? Everyone should have one. (Rosette's is marked as her V.S.P. on the map on page 11.)

In the days that followed, Rosette often returned to her 'Very Special Place' and spent many joy-filled hours there.

Sometimes while lying on the moss she'd look up and smile at the fluffy cloud-mice that drifted through the sky. Sometimes she would visit with the local rabbits and birds to learn more about her new home.

And, sometimes - Rosette *sang*.

Yes, she sang.

Now, Dear Reader, most likely you were unaware that field-mice can sing. Few people *are* aware of this. But, it is, in fact, quite *real*. Field-mice *do* sing. (You can read more about singing mice on page 231.)

It was on the second or third day after Rosette had listened to Wren playing her flute - the second or third day since she had found her 'Very Special Place' - that Rosette started humming the tune Wren had played for her – the one from the Gnomes' Thanks-Giving Celebration.

As she slowly started to remember the words she'd heard them sing that night, she, Rosette the mouse, started to sing the song.

♪ "We give thanks. We give thanks… La-la-la…. ♪ Mmm, now what were those words?" she asked herself.

"Oh, yes, that's right… ♪ Summer is gone, autumn is here - soon it will be cold!" ♪

Over and over she sang the as she twirled about. Her voice rang out, sweet and pure.

She sang it again and again. And then she added her *own words*.

It was just at that very moment that Hummy happened to fly into the Commons.

(Although bees don't collect much nectar in the late autumn, Hummy still had considerable work to do for the hive. And as we all know how dedicated Hummy was to helping her Queen Bee.)

When she heard the mysterious singing she circled around and around the meadow trying to find its source.

"Surely it was a *fairy* I just heard singing…" Hummy thought to herself.

And then she spied Rosette half hidden in her grassy bower.

"Oh, hello, Rosette," she said. "Say, did you just hear someone singing? I think there must be a fairy nearby!" It never occurred to Hummy that it could have been a *mouse* who had been singing.

"Oh, hello, Hummy! I hope my singing didn't bother you," Rosette replied innocently.

"That was *you* singing? Why, why that was *beautiful!* Oh, please sing some more."

But just as Rosette began her song again Hummy interrupted her.

"No, no, wait, Rosette! I have an idea! Please, stay right here and don't move. I will be right back. *Please, please* Rosette, don't go anywhere," said Hummy anxiously before buzzing off.

Hummy had decided that she *must* tell everyone else to come and hear her singing too. (My, my, Hummy was almost as thoughtful as a gnome, wasn't she?)

Hummy probably would have rung the Ding-Dong to announce her discovery, but then, she was only a bee and the clapper to the Ding-Dong *was* very heavy. Besides the sound it made might have frightened Rosette away!'

Hummy quickly buzzed all over the woods to locate as many of her friends as she could. When she excitedly told them that she had discovered a 'Wonder in the Commons' and that they all must come, each stopped what they were doing and hurried there.

Of course, Hummy didn't bother Pebble, since he was probably sound asleep after his night's work.

And Mossy and Brother Acorn were off someplace or other. But Wren, Gilly and Teasel and Tweed came right away to see what it was that Hummy was buzzing so enthusiastically about.

When the gnomes gathered in the Commons they were surprised to find Mother Comfrey had arrived there as well.

Mother Comfrey seemed to always have the habit of showing up at *just the right time*. Sometimes it was when she sensed someone was ill or hurt. Sometimes it was just before something *important* was about to happen. But why she had come at this particular moment was a mystery.

The gnomes silently hailed each other as they tiptoed in quietly circling around the source of the mysterious singing they heard.

And then they saw Little Rosette.

There she was wearing her new sweater. Her eyes were closed. She was holding onto a stem of grass while standing on her hind legs and gently swaying. And she was *singing*.

Hushed, and in awe, the gnomes stood there and listened.

♪ "I give thanks, I give thanks, for *all my friends*. Summer is gone - autumn is here. Soon it will be cold." ♪

Upon hearing that, the gnomes gaped. "Mice can *sing?*" they wondered.

When she repeated the song, with her special words added, "I give thanks, for *all my friends*," the gnomes smiled. Then quietly, at first, so as not to frighten her, they all joined in and sang together.

♪ "We give thanks, we give thanks, *for our Dear Rosette*. Summer is gone - autumn is here. Soon it will be cold." ♪

Of course, when Rosette heard the other's voices, she stopped singing at once and opened her eyes. Can you imagine how astonished she must have been to find so many of her new friends circled around her?

When Mother Comfrey saw how surprised Rosette was, she stepped towards her and said, "Oh, Dear, Dear Little Rosette. Thank you. Thank you!

"What a beautiful voice you have. What a special *gift* that is! Don't you agree, friends?" she said gesturing to the others.

The other gnomes just beamed in amazement at the mouse.

"And, we are all very glad to have you as a friend *too*, Rosette," stated Gilly in response to the words Rosette had added to her song. Clearly, he was voicing the thoughts of the other gnomes there, for all nodded and smiled in agreement.

Then Mother Comfrey turned to the others and said, "Friends, we have all enjoyed a very special treat this afternoon. May I suggest that you take the sweet memory of this little mouse's song with you when you return to your homes? I wish to talk with Rosette."

The gnomes all called out their 'thanks' and 'goodbyes' to the mouse, and to Mother Comfrey as well, and went their ways.

Hummy, too, very anxious to tell her Queen all about what had just happened, quickly returned to the Royal Hive.

17.
A Gift

When they were finally alone, Mother Comfrey said to the mouse, "Rosette, do you know what we gnomes believe the *most* important thing in life is?"

The mouse shook her head, for she had no idea at all. Do you, Reader?

"We believe that it is to discover what our *gift* is. For when we find out what our *gift* is, (that special thing is that we can do, that we love to do), only then will we be able to *give it back* to the world - to help others."

Reader, did you understand what Mother Comfrey just said? If not, you might want to discuss it with your parents or guardian.

"Now, here you are," she continued, "a very sweet, very young, and very small field-mouse who happens to have a very *special gift*.

My Dear Rosette, even though you are not a gnome, I believe that if you have a special gift like that, like your lovely voice - you *must* find ways to use it!"

Now, Reader ever since the moment that Rosette discovered she had an audience while she was singing - ever since Mother Comfrey had spoken to the group and ever since they had all returned to their homes, our Rosette had *yet* to say a single word!

"But, but, what do you mean 'it's my *gift*,' Mother Comfrey?" Rosette uttered at last. "I don't understand."

"Oh, dear, of course, you don't. Whatever was I thinking?" she asked, more to herself than to the mouse.

"Rosette, I would like to take you back to Mossy's now. May I do that?" said Mother Comfrey after a moment.

When the mouse agreed, Mother Comfrey scooped Rosette up into her loving arms and placed her on the seat of her wagon. Then, urging Hasa, to lead the way, they headed south towards Mossy's house.

As they made their way through the woods, Mother Comfrey looked down at the mouse and said, "How are you enjoying being in Limindoor, Rosette?"

"Oh, I am *so* happy here, Mother Comfrey. Everyone is so very nice!"

Mother Comfrey smiled at that. Then, after a moment she said, "Dear, I want you to do something. I want you to think about this lovely sweater and how it makes you feel. Did Teasel and Tweed give it to you?"

"No, Mother Comfrey, it was Meggy!"

"Meggy, you say? My! My! What nice knitting!

"Well, I want you to think about how *warm* your sweater feels on you. I want you to think about the *love* Meggy must have felt giving it to you. And I want you to think about how *good* that love feels. It's a lot more than *just a sweater* now, isn't it?" she asked.

Rosette thought about what she had said and nodded, "Uh, huh."

"Your singing is like that. Your singing is much more than just a song; which was very sweet, by the way. It is about the *love* that is *in* your song.

"Your *singing* is your gift, Rosette. When you give it to others it is the same as you lovingly giving someone a warm sweater," said Mother Comfrey as Hasa pulled the carriage up to Mossy's yard.

"Now, hop down, Little One, and go inside to your Mossy. I will be seeing you soon."

Rosette gave Mother Comfrey a hug and then jumped down and scampered along Mossy's path as the carriage pulled away.

Rosette found Mossy sitting in his usual place on the bench in front of his house. He was holding his Bearberry pipe, but it was unlit (which was quite unusual for him.)

Actually, Mossy looked kind of blue. (No, not the color blue, Reader, but the *mood* blue.) He looked sad and very alone.

Rosette stopped at his feet, looked up at him and said, "I am sorry I was gone so long, Mossy."

"Oh, that's okay, Mees. Did you have a good time on your walk?" was his reply.

Now, Reader, did you catch what he said? Do you understand why he said it? He called Rosette, *Mees*. Why would he do that, do you think? If you thought it was because Mossy was missing his old friend, then you were correct.

Mossy wasn't even aware he had said what he said. But Rosette was. Yet, she didn't correct him. She simply said, "I had a good time, Mossy."

Rosette might not have been all that wise, but she was very sensitive for being such a young little mouse. She could tell that Mossy was still so very sad and she so wished that she could do something to make him feel better.

When she reached up to put a comforting paw on his knee she happened to glance at the fuzzy sleeve of her sweater. That reminded her of what Mother Comfrey had just been saying about her gift.

"I wonder…," she thought to herself.

She paused and then, very softly and sweetly, Rosette started to sing to Mossy.

She sang him a pure wordless song; a song both tender and simple.

At first, the sound of her voice startled Mossy. He too did not know that mice could sing… surely none of his companions had *ever* sung to him in the past. But then he calmly sat back and listened.

Mossy listened as her sweet, loving, melody sounded out into the late afternoon.

As he sat there listening, he took a deep, deep breath.

When he let it out, he noticed something magical happen to him. All of the pain and sadness he had been feeling from missing Mees so much seemed to just …blow away.

Mossy looked down at that curious, pale little mouse in her comical sweater; that little mouse who was singing his troubles away, and he smiled.

After she had finished her song, Mossy turned to her again and said, "Thank you for that, Little Rosette! Thank you so, so much."

And he reached down and tenderly picked her up and carried her into their home.

18.
A Dream

Autumn brought many changes to Limindoor - as well as many changes to the lives of Gus and Meggy. Now, instead of spending endless summer days with the gnomes, they spent most of their days in school.

On the weekdays they both still had to get up at dawn in order to finish their chores. But instead of meeting later in Limindoor Woods, they'd meet on the path behind Apple Tree Hill and together, head east across the meadow for the long walk to their single room schoolhouse.

It was Monday, the day after Gus and Meggy's sojourn across Muddy Brook and their meeting with Master Kruk.

Gus had awakened early from a very strange dream. Images from the dream kept flitting through his mind all morning. They were there as he chopped wood for the stove, as he checked to see if the hens had laid any eggs, and as he spread a blanket of fallen leaves over the garden beds. Even while he ate his breakfast he was distracted by thoughts of his dream. This continued even later when he met up with Meggy.

Reader, have you ever experienced that - when bits and pieces of a dream you just had keep on dancing around in your mind?

After the two children had walked together for some distance and Gus had yet to say a single word, Meggy finally blurted out, "Gus, what *is* it that's *bothering* you?"

"What? Oh, gosh, Meggy. I am sorry. It's just that… well; I had the oddest dream last night. I am still trying to figure it out," Gus admitted.

"Why don't you tell me about it?" she said as they climbed over the stile. (A stile is a step device that you can climb on to easily get over a fence. They had to cross two of them on the way to school every day.)

"Well, I can only remember parts of it.

"Let me see… there were people, lots of people, and they were standing up on a high ledge looking across a canyon to another ledge. They were trying to get to the other side, but couldn't. Then I came along. I was big; I mean *really, really tall*. I was so tall that when I leaned over I could take ahold of that other ledge. And when I did that all the people walked *across my back* to get to the other side."

"Your back?" asked Meggy making a funny face.

"Yup! See, didn't I tell you it was a strange dream?"

"Dreams are often strange, Gus," replied Meggy, wisely.

"You know," she said after a moment. "The first thing your dream made me think of was how *big* we are when compared to our friends in Limindoor. I bet they are actually pretty *small* if we saw them out of Limindoor!"

"Mmm, yeah, you are right," said Gus and he continued to mull over what she'd said as they walked on in silence.

"Oh, look, there are the Larson twins!" Meggy cried out when she spied two of their classmates crossing the field. "I'll see you later, Gus," she said as she eagerly dashed ahead to greet them.

The children's teacher kept them busy with many interesting things to learn and think about at school. At the end of the day, the students always had chores to do before going home. Gus's job was to refill the water barrel with drinking water. Meggy's job was to sweep the classroom.

Just as they were finishing up, Gus happened to look over at Meggy and saw her playfully balancing her broom between two of the desks. Suddenly, he got an idea!

"That's *it*, Meggy!" Gus suddenly exclaimed. "My dream! A *bridge*. I was a *bridge* in my dream!"

Meggy's mouth formed a little O. "Are you thinking what I am thinking, Gus?" she asked.

"Shh! Let's talk about it on the way home," Gus whispered.

Now, Reader, if you have read the other stories about Limindoor Woods then you'll know that Gus's family knew *all about* the gnomes who lived there. But, as to his teacher or even their classmates knowing about them, well, Gus and Meggy had decided that they'd keep that part of their lives to themselves. Though they'd never keep secrets from their parents, they didn't think that *everyone else* had to know about the gnomes.

And, why bring up the gnomes at this point, you may ask? Well, both Gus and Meggy realized at once that the bridge of Gus's dream must have been a bridge *for the gnomes*. Remember? In Gus's dream, he had been so much larger than the people he had helped.

And they both realized at once that Gus's dream must have also been about him *building* a bridge for the gnomes of Limindoor Woods.

They couldn't wait till it was time to shake their teacher's hand to say 'goodbye' and head back toward home.

"A gnome bridge! A gnome bridge!" they sang later as they skipped along the path.

Suddenly Meggy stopped. "But a bridge from *where*? To *where*?" she asked.

"Where else, but a bridge across Muddy Brook?" was Gus's reply.

"Of course!" agreed Meggy excitedly.

They walked on for a while deep in thought. Suddenly Gus burst out, "Master Kruk!"

"What about Master Kruk?" she asked.

"The nails! Remember, he gave me those building-nails? Maybe he wanted me to use them to make a bridge."

"Do you really think that that was what he was 'caw-cawing' about, Gus?" she asked.

"Oh, I don't know. But, won't it be fun to build a bridge? You'll help me, won't you, Meggy?" Gus asked generously.

"I've never built a bridge before, Gus," she admitted. "Isn't it kind of a *big* project?"

"Well, that's just it, Meggy. It won't be all *that big* of a project because we will be building it for the gnomes - who are small.

"Oh, how I wish it were Friday, Meggy. Now we'll have to wait *all week* before we can start building. At least I'll have time to figure out how I'm going to do it," said Gus.

After walking and thinking a while, Gus said, "I am going to run on ahead, Meggy, if that's okay. I have things to figure out. I'll see you tomorrow!" And he dashed off.

He was so inspired; his mind was just racing with ideas.

19.
The Builders

What excitement! Gus hardly slept that night. He had so many thoughts milling around in his mind.

How big would the bridge have to be? How would he build it? What tools would he need?

He wished he could remember how wide the stream was. If only he could go back to visit the stream he would know more. The questions kept coming.

Perhaps, Reader, you are wondering *why* he didn't quickly run over to the other side of Limindoor to take measurements - so that he could plan it all out. Well, first of all, he had agreed to his parents that once school had started he wouldn't go into the woods on weekdays.

And, even if he had been allowed to, it would have taken way too long.

For, though the distance *to* Limindoor was not far at all, once he was inside and had become very small, the distance inside would have *become much larger.* It would have taken him quite a long time to cross Limindoor. That, plus the days growing shorter with winter approaching, it would have made a trip there and back before dark practically impossible.

Even though he was kept busy with chores and school work, Gus did find some time over the next few days to sketch out a simple bridge. And he got permission from his father to borrow the hatchet. (A hatchet is like a little ax that has a flat edge on its head that could be used like a hammer.) His father also gave him some more nails to add to those Master Kruk had given him.

Gus planned to meet Meggy bright and early on Saturday and together they would head west through Limindoor.

They hoped there'd be no problem passing through the barrier and becoming full size again, as they had done before.

At last, it was dawn. Gus quickly dressed, as always, in his knee-high pants, button down shirt and vest. He tied on his low boots and, now that it was colder, he also put on a heavy woolen short-coat.

After doing his chores of chopping up enough wood for the kitchen stove, he found the sheath (or case) for the hatchet so he could carry it safely in the bottom of his bag.

His thoughtful mother had kindly given him a small lunch of bread, cheese to take with him. Gus was all set to go!

Meggy was also just as excited about the outing.

She'd always loved building little fairy houses out of twigs and such. But she had never built anything as grand as a bridge before.

She had no idea what she could bring that would be of help to Gus. So she brought something that she was pretty sure he would enjoy; a batch of Apple Jackets.

Reader, you should know that Meggy's Apple Jackets were renowned throughout Limindoor. An Apple Jacket is an apple that has been cored, filled with raisins and nuts and spices, then wrapped in pastry and baked. Yum, yum!

Meggy tied her apron over her full, calf-length dress. Her apron had large pockets in which she usually carried a ball of yarn, for Meggy's hands were rarely idle. Now that it was late autumn she put on a dress-length wool coat. Her only shoes were brown lace-up high-top boots. She'd be in need of a new pair soon, as she was growing so quickly.

Meggy packed the Apple Jackets in her basket along with a small lunch. Usually, when she was in Limindoor she shared lunch with the Knitting Gnomes.

But this time she knew she would be off in the country with Gus and they would have to fend for themselves.

The two children met at Meggy's portal; a small opening in a tangle of bracken, just south of her home where her father's field bordered with the woods. Though they had to almost crawl to enter it, the two soon found themselves in a high, spacious clearing under a canopy of great trees. Of course, they and all they were carrying had shrunk to gnome size.

The two children crossed Limindoor in record time having decided not to visit any of their gnome friends that day. When they got to the fern bower, Gus removed his hat. And when they stepped under the ferns, their feet slipped once again on the gravel at the bank of the stream and they knew they had become full sized Tall Ones yet again.

20.
The Bridge

After putting down their things on the meadow side of Muddy Brook, the children went about with their building preparations.

Gus's plan (a rather good one too) was to find the narrowest part of the stream and to measure its distance across. Meggy offered her yarn for that. Then they would go to the old oak tree with all of its fallen branches and see if they could find lengths of wood that were suitable to span the creek.

The two main beams would have to be long and sturdy enough for the job - and would have to be a similar shape to each other as well. The shorter cross-pieces would be much easier to find, as would the stout slabs of bark they'd use to 'pave' the bridge.

Master Kruk, the crow, greeted them with great enthusiasm when he saw the children arrive. It was almost as though he had been waiting for them.

It took a while to locate the two main cross beams, drag them to the stream and for Gus to chop away the unnecessary parts. By the time they had placed the beams so that they spanned from one side of the stream to the other, and had firmly anchored them there with rocks, the two children were ready for a break.

With winter was on the way, it was a very chilly day. But when the children sat on a log to share their late morning snack, they found a bit of warmth from the thin sunshine.

Soon Master Kruk flew over to join them and gave Gus a couple more nails to use on his project. And in exchange, he was given one of Meggy's Apple Jackets to eat.

"You know what we are doing, don't you, Master Kruk?" Gus asked of him pointing over to the beginnings of the bridge.

"Caw-caw, caw-caw! Caw! Caw! Caw!" replied the crow, bobbing his shiny beak up and down.

Master Kruk could understand the children. But as they were outside of the magic of Limindoor, the children could not understand his reply.

"We had better get to work, Meggy," said Gus packing up the remainder of his lunch. "We still have a lot to do."

"Sure, and while you are working on the bridge, Gus, I want to go gather some moss from along the stream's bank," said Meggy.

They had decided that they would wedge moss between the cracks of the bark pavement to smooth out the surface.

Meggy emptied her basket to use it for gathering the moss. And Gus went off to cut the cross pieces and to find some slabs of bark to 'pave' the bridge.

Reader, this might be the right time to give you a better idea of the size of the project they had undertaken.

Though you have surely seen bridges before, it is doubtful that you have ever seen one like the one Gus and Meggy were building.

The stream, Muddy Brook, at its narrowest point was only a bit wider than a grownup's arm span. Gus had found two stout branches that reached from one side of the stream bank to the other. When in place the two formed a gentle rise in the middle of the stream.

Since they were making the bridge for the *gnomes* to cross, the width of the bridge surface did not need to be so very wide.

Actually, most likely the bridge would only be used by Mother Comfrey crossing it on her wagon, as the other gnomes rarely left Limindoor.

So Gus had settled on making it about two feet wide.

21.
Uh, oh!

With her basket in hand, Meggy slowly made her way north along the meadow-side bank of the stream.

She had no desire to unintentionally become gnome-sized while there was Tall One's work to do. Had she been on the Limindoor side there would always have been a chance of her accidentally stepping through a portal.

Meggy soon arrived at a point where the stream curved off to the left. When she looked behind her she could no longer see Gus. But, just up ahead she did spy exactly what she wanted! There she could see that the stream bank was *carpeted* with masses of lush green moss.

To reach the moss, though, Meggy had to get around a thick old tree branch that reached out over the water.

She saw there were several dry stepping stones scattered across the stream there, so she carefully held onto a bush with her free hand, and stepped out onto one of the stones.

Uh, oh! When she stepped on the stone, it shifted under her foot, and down went Meggy with a *splash!!!*

Now, don't worry, Reader, the stream was not very deep. So, on that account Meggy was fine. But she did get *wet* - soaked, in fact. By the time Meggy had righted herself onto a sturdier stone and recovered her basket, (which had quickly started to fill with water,) she found that she was sodden - through and through.

Meggy attempted to wring out her skirt and coat hems as best she could before she quickly gathered the treasure of moss she'd spied. When she had collected a good amount, she climbed up over the bank, through some bushes, and onto the meadow.

"Hi, Gus," she called as she approached him. "Look at all this wonderful moss I found!"

Gus grinned at her from the middle of his bridge. He was feeling very proud of his work, for it had all come together just as he'd planned. He even risked to make a little jump on the span where he stood and was greatly relieved that it all held firmly together.

"Will it hold me too?" Meggy asked.

"Sure, come on up," he called.

It was only when Meggy took his hand to join him on the bridge that Gus got a good look at her.

"What's wrong with you, Meggy? Your lips are… why they are *blue!*"

Meggy shuttered with the cold and admitted, "Silly me, I slipped into the stream. I'm okay, though."

"You mean you are all *wet*? But Meggy, it's so cold today!"

"Really, I am alright," she said. But her chattering teeth belied her words.

Gus reached over and felt her wrist. It was icy. "No, you're not alright! We better get you home *right away*. You have to get warmed up. Come on. We can finish the bridge another time. Now, where are your things?"

It is possible, Reader, that you might be thinking that Gus had responded in a very *grown-up* manner to Meggy's plight. Indeed, there are *few* Tall Ones of his age who would have paid much attention to how cold *either* of them was… particularly a child so engaged in an exciting building project like theirs. But once again, you must remember that Gus was dedicated to becoming a Gentle-gnome. And being so, he strove to always follow the Way of Gnome in exercising *kindness*. (Well done, Gus!)

Meggy soon realized that she really was pretty uncomfortable.

Her teeth just wouldn't stop chattering, so she nodded in agreement that they should go.

Gus promptly emptied the moss from Meggy's basket into a pile on the stream bank. He then gathered her things into the basket, grabbed it and swung his own packed bag over his shoulder before taking her icy hand. In no time the two of them had quickly crossed back into the magic of Limindoor Woods.

To be honest, that was probably the only time that Gus ever *regretted* the magic of Limindoor. For, had they been full sized Tall Ones then, they could have crossed the woods in minutes. But since they had become gnome-sized, the distance they had to travel had become far greater.

And, as Limindoor was mostly forest, the only real sunshine they encountered there was when they crossed the Commons.

Coldness is a strange thing. You would think that since they were moving as fast as they were that the activity would have warmed Meggy.

But, unfortunately, the icy dampness of her clothing had chilled her to the bone. As much as she tried, she was unable to stop trembling.

Had the two been really smart they would have stopped at one of the gnome's houses to get Meggy warmed up. But Gus, feeling responsible for Meggy, had only one thought in his mind, that he had to get her back to her mother and *quickly*!

At last, they slipped through Meggy's portal and together ran towards her home.

When Meggy's mother saw her condition, Meggy was immediately sent upstairs to get out of her wet clothes and to get into bed.

Gus apologized profusely for what had happened. To which Meggy's mother sensibly said that she well understood how accidents could happen and thanked him for bringing Meggy back so quickly.

When Gus left Meggy's house he was all at odds with himself. He wasn't sure what to do. There wasn't really enough time to go all that distance back through the woods to work on the bridge, so instead, he turned towards home.

To the south, in the distance, he could see his favorite tree up on top of Apple Tree hill. So he decided to go climb the tree and sit a while and think.

Outside of being in Limindoor Woods, Gus considered that high perch in the apple tree his favorite place to be; his Very Special Place. For from there he could see most of the countryside.

Actually, it was from that tree that he had *first* spied Star Mountain. And it was his curiosity about that mountain that had brought him to eventually discover the magic of Limindoor Woods.

When Gus finally climbed to the top of the hill, after leaving Meggy's, he found that the tree was bare of leaves and there were only a few stalwart apples hanging from its remotest branches. He decided that he liked it best that way.

The very first time he had climbed up in the tree had been that summer, soon after his family had moved into the little Red and White house that he now called home.

He had discovered a comfortable roost high up there in a private leafy-green hideaway. From there he could look out over the meadow and at the strange, high dark forest he later learned was Limindoor Woods. But now, with the leaves gone, he could see in *all* directions.

Isn't it wonderful, Reader, how our eyes can 'take' us to such distant places, just by our looking?

Now, once again in the tree Gus looked out across the meadow and saw a distant crow swooping in wide lazy circles in the sky. He thought of Master Kruk. And that made him think of the bridge he had just built.

Gus felt very good about what he had done. He had never built anything like that before. It's true, it wasn't really all that big, but he had tested it and it was sturdy.

"It was too bad that they hadn't been able to finish it," he thought; "too bad that they hadn't placed the moss in the cracks between the bark. What if Mother Comfrey were to discover the bridge the way they left it? What a bumpy ride she would have!"

But Gus needn't have worried. And you will hear why.

When Master Kruk had seen the children hastily leave Muddy Brook, he went to explore the work they had been doing. He hopped up on the bridge, pecked at the bark pavers and found them solid. Yes, he approved of that boy's work.

Now, Reader, you must know that crows are very intelligent creatures. They have been credited with doing any number of amazing things – using tools, solving puzzles, and such. And, it is true that Master Kruk was a quite exceptional crow - as far as crows go. So, when he saw that pile of moss that the children had left near the bridge, it took hardly a moment for the bird to figure out what was for.

His beak, it so happened, was the perfect tool for the job. In no time he'd carefully wedged clods of moss between the cracks of the bark pavers, finishing off the job that Meggy had meant to do.

"Yes, indeed, it was a good thing that young Gus had listened to me about building this bridge," thought the crow to himself. "Mother Comfrey will be most pleased with it, too!"

22.
The Offering

The next day Gus went to Meggy's house early eagerly expecting she'd want to come with him to finish the work on the bridge.

Meggy's mother wearily answered the door saying that Meggy had become quite ill over the night. She'd slept very poorly, developed a sore throat and a high fever and was now complaining of a painful earache. "I am afraid she won't be going anywhere for a while, Gus," Meggy's mother said worriedly.

Poor Gus, he still felt so responsible. If only they had just stayed in the woods this wouldn't have happened.

Reader, it is important for you to know that her just getting so chilled is *not* what caused Meggy's illness.

Actually, Gus and Meggy were very healthy children. Living in the country, enjoying all of that fresh air, and eating wholesome food are all things that can make and keep you healthy. No, it wasn't because of the icy water – it was more likely something she had caught elsewhere that had caused being sick. Her getting so chilled might have just made it harder to fight it off the illness. There is no way to be sure.

But, whatever caused it, Meggy was now sadly very sick. And there was no saying how long it would take for her to get better.

Gus said he was so sorry to hear about his friend and offered to help in any way he could. But Meggy's mother thanked him with a tired smile and said, "We just want her to get better, Gus. That's all; we just want her to *heal*."

When she mentioned 'healing,' the first person Gus thought of was, of course, Mother Comfrey!

He knew he must go find her right away. So he quickly said goodbye to Meggy's mama and promised to return the next day. Then he made his way directly to Meggy's portal and into Limindoor to find the Healing Gnome. Surely she would be able to help Meggy - if anyone could.

The first one to meet him when he got to the main path in the woods was Hummy.

"There you are, Gus," she buzzed excitedly. "Mother Comfrey is looking for you. You can find her in the Commons. Where is Meggy today?" asked the bee.

"Oh! Hello, Hummy. You say Mother Comfrey is looking for *me*? That's funny, *I* am looking for *her!*

"And as to Meggy, she isn't feeling well at all today, that's why I wanted Mother Comfrey," he said as the two headed back towards the Commons.

When they arrived Gus found Mother Comfrey deep in conversation with that little mouse, Rosette.

As you may have guessed, Mother Comfrey had somehow *sensed* that Gus had need of her. And even though, at the time, she had been far off to the west of Limindoor visiting with Master Kruk, she had come as soon as she could.

And, yes, she *had* crossed over Gus's bridge. In fact, Master Kruk had just been telling her how hard the children had worked on the bridge. And she'd been most curious to see it.

Master Kruk was quite proud of the fact that it was *he* who had had the idea that the children build the bridge for her. He knew it would be much easier for Tall Ones to build it than the gnomes. And he was glad, too, that he had been able to communicate the idea of building it to Gus when the children had visited him the week before.

Now, Reader, isn't it interesting that Master Kruk believed all *that*, and Gus and Meggy believed *something else* entirely?

So, now back to Mother Comfrey...

She *had* just crossed the bridge on her way to see Gus and greatly admired the work the children had done on it. When she entered the Commons she discovered young Rosette playing there and stopped for a quick chat.

Of course when she saw Hummy buzzing by Mother Comfrey alerted the bee that she was looking for Gus.

But when Gus arrived it was Rosette who saw him first. "Hello Gus," she said smiling as she scampered up to him. "I still use the ramp you made me. I use it *all* the time!"

"Why, hello to you, Rosette," he replied with a smile. "I am glad you like it!

"Good morning, Mother Comfrey," he said, turning to her.

"Good day, Gus. I want to thank you for that *wonderful* bridge. Master Kruk told me you built it. What a thoughtful and useful gift! I just now crossed it to get here - it made my journey so much shorter."

"Oh, you are welcome, Mother Comfrey," said Gus with an odd combination of pride and shyness.

"It was fun to build. But, I didn't do it by myself. Meggy helped me. Actually, it is about Meggy that I wanted to see you."

"Yes, I thought so," replied the old gnome. Mother Comfrey did indeed have the uncanny ability to sense whenever any of her friends needed her.

"What is the problem, Gus?" she asked with concern.

"I just went to visit her and her mother said that she was *really sick*. Oh, I feel so bad for her, Mother Comfrey. You see, she fell into the stream…."

"Meggy is *sick*, you say? Oh, dear, that's not good!"

"Can you help her, Mother Comfrey?"

"Well, I don't know, Gus. The fact that Meggy lives *outside* of Limindoor could pose quite a problem," she replied with concern.

All the time that Mother Comfrey and Gus were talking, little Rosette was standing between them looking first up at one and then the other.

"Excuse me, excuse me. Mother Comfrey. Excuse me, Gus. I don't mean to interrupt. But, did I hear you say that Meggy is sick?" Rosette asked with concern.

"Apparently she is, Little One," said Mother Comfrey.

"But you can get her better, can't you, Mother Comfrey?" said the mouse. "You can fix *anyone!* That's what all the animals here tell me!"

"She's right, isn't she, Mother Comfrey? You can heal her, can't you?" begged Gus.

"Well, my dears, it isn't quite as easy as that. If she were a gnome or an animal, I would say "yes", for I probably could. But Meggy is a Tall One. She is from another world - your world, Gus."

Gus suddenly brightened up and asked, "I know, Mother Comfrey, what about the *Silver Spring*?"

Hidden at the base of Star Mountain was the Silver Spring, an enchanted spring with special healing waters. Gus had accidentally discovered it that summer when he had been off exploring the woods. It was Mother Comfrey who had shown him how powerful the waters were when she used them to cure Mossy the time he had eaten some bad berries.

"I am sorry, Gus, but unfortunately, the magic of Silver Spring will only work *inside* of Limindoor Woods," she explained.

Poor Gus, he had been so filled with hope. Now he was so disappointed that he actually looked deflated. But he was also angry, angry with himself. He still blamed himself for Meggy being sick.

"I am sorry Gus, truly sorry. If I can think of anything to do for her, I promise I will.

After a moment Mother Comfrey seeing how disturbed Gus was, wisely suggested that he go visit his Gnome-papa. "I think he is the best person for you to see right now. I really do."

Gus nodded in agreement and mumbled his goodbyes before he turned to the path that would lead him to Mossy's.

On his way there, Gus realized that there was really nowhere else he would rather be than visiting with his Gnomepapa. It had been far too long since he had done so and so *much* had happened since then.

Meanwhile, Little Rosette was standing completely still, right there in the middle of the Commons, with her eyes closed. After Gus had left, Mother Comfrey turned to see the mouse and asked with great concern, "What is it, Rosette? Whatever is wrong, child?"

After a moment the mouse opened her eyes and said, "It's Meggy, Mother Comfrey. *I* want to help her. You said that she is sick…and that there was nothing *you* can do.

"I have a *gift*, you said so yourself. Can't *I* use my gift to make her better?"

Mother Comfrey was stunned that she would say such a thing. "You mean you wish to *sing* to Meggy, Rosette?" she asked.

"Yes! You told me my singing was my *gift*... my gift to *give*! I want to give it to Meggy! I want her to get all better. Oh, please, Mother Comfrey! Please!" she begged.

"Oh, dear, dear Little Rosette, you do have so much *love* in you. But, I don't know. Going to her home could be so very dangerous.

"You know that Meggy is really a Tall One, Rosette. She is only gnome-sized when she is in Limindoor Woods. And, also, she lives *outside* of Limindoor. In a house, yet! And, besides that, I recall that her family has a *cat*!"

Rosette stared up at Mother Comfrey as she listened to her. Her eyes were wide and unblinking. When Mother Comfrey finished what she was saying, Rosette informed her,

"That's okay. My mother taught me how to get inside of Tall One's buildings…

"And as to the cat…" she said shuddering slightly. "I can be careful. Oh, please, please," she begged again. "I *really* want to do this."

Though Mother Comfrey had been a healer for a very long time she had never encountered a situation quite like this. Even with all of her herbs and magic, she could not think of how she herself could ever help Meggy; her being a Tall One.

And now she was faced with this little mouse who had a very different kind of healing magic - her voice. Mother Comfrey was fully aware how powerful the magic of Rosette's voice was - for she was certain it was that which had so helped Mossy with his grieving.

"But how, how could Rosette ever get close enough to Meggy for her magic to work?" she wondered. Mother Comfrey would have to meditate on it. Maybe, just maybe, there was an answer.

"Dear one, go on home now," she said at last to the mouse. "I need some time to think about this. I will be there shortly.

"For right now though please, don't say anything about this to Mossy. I will talk to him myself when I arrive."

When she said that, Rosette joyfully tried to jump up into the old gnome's arms.

Mother Comfrey had been so right when she'd said that the mouse had "so much love in her."

"Oh, thank you, thank you Mother Comfrey! I know there is a way. I just know it. There *has* to be.

"Why else would I have this gift, unless I can give it? You will think of a way. You are Mother Comfrey," said the mouse as she nuzzled the gnome's hand.

"I will go home now like you asked me to. I love you, Mother Comfrey," she said.

Then the little mouse left the old gnome and scurried as best as she could back to Mossy's.

23.
A Request

Mossy and Gus were working together out in the yard when Mother Comfrey's wagon finally arrived. The two of them were carefully picking pine-nuts out of several pinecones that Mossy had found. After they finished, they planned on packing the nuts into acorn jars, to store for the winter.

Being such a wise and loving Gentle-gnome, Mossy had noticed right away how muddled Gus seemed when he showed up. He didn't know what Gus's problem was but he did know that the best thing for someone in that condition was to get him busy with some kind of work… thus the task of picking and packing pine-nuts.

When Little Rosette had arrived she also seemed to be in some kind of a mood.

She was milling about the yard quietly mumbling to herself. Mossy, not knowing her as well as he did Gus, decided to just let her be for a while.

"Hello, hello, you busy ones," said Mother Comfrey as she climbed down from her wagon. "Ah, it looks like you have quite a treasure trove of pine-nuts here!" she exclaimed when she saw their work.

Then turning to Mossy, she asked right away, "Mossy, my friend, may I please have a moment to speak with you?"

"Certainly, certainly! Mother Comfrey. Why don't you come inside with me and we will have some tea?

"And thank you for your help here," he said turning to Gus. "I am going to visit with Mother Comfrey. Do you mind continuing with these pine-nuts until I return to join you?"

With Gus's nod of agreement, Mossy led Mother Comfrey into his tiny home.

Mother Comfrey had gone to Mossy's only after she had finally come up with a plan for Meggy. The plan had not come to her easily.

When Rosette had left her earlier, Mother Comfrey had climbed up into the caravan. (Can you imagine, Reader, what it would be like to always have your own little home with you at all times?) Once inside she sat down at her little table, lit an acorn-cap candle and became very still.

She tried to clear her head of the clutter of her thoughts; thoughts about poor Meggy, about how impossible it seemed that that little mouse could somehow get to Meggy to help her, thoughts about the dangers she could meet on the way.

It took her some time, but when her mind was finally clear she was able to find the peace to consider all of the options.

Soon she came to realize that it *could actually* be possible, that Rosette *could actually* safely get to see Meggy. And, best of all, that there seemed that there was a chance that Rosette *could* very feasibly cure the girl.

Mother Comfrey sat a while longer until she knew just what must be done. Then she snuffed the candle, exited her little room, climbed up onto the bench of her wagon and made her way to Mossy's.

"Mossy," Mother Comfrey said as she sat at his table and took a sip of dewdrop tea. "I have an unusual favor to ask of you. I wish to 'borrow' young Rosette for a while."

Mossy, though surprised by her request, had such faith in his friend, that the thought of refusing her never crossed his mind.

"Certainly, Mother Comfrey. How long will you need her for?" he asked.

Now that Mossy had suddenly started feeling less pain about his loss of his beloved Mees he found that his caring for little Rosette was growing leaps and bounds.

"Thank you, old friend. I knew I could count on you. I am not certain how long we will be. I might return her tonight - or possibly even tomorrow. There is something very important she wishes to do. She is going to help me with a 'healing' matter."

"Ah, then you will want to take this for her," he said as he stood, retrieved Rosette's fuzzy blanket and handed it to the old gnome. "She can't sleep at night without it. The other night when she misplaced it she had an awful time until we finally found it hidden under the bed! Sometimes that mouse seems so old and wise. And other times she seems such a child."

When they went outside Mossy called to Rosette who immediately rushed to his side.

"Rosette, Mother Comfrey has told me that she would like to take you somewhere.

Do you wish to go with her?" Mossy felt that the choice was really up to her, after all.

Rosette first beamed at Mother Comfrey and then turned to Mossy before answering very mysteriously, "Oh, yes, I *so* want to help in any way that I can, Mossy. I *do* want to go. I do! I do!"

That settled it. Mossy leaned down to give Rosette a loving goodbye hug and said, "Take care of her, Mother Comfrey. She has become very dear to me."

Gus had overheard very little of what they were saying but hoped that Mother Comfrey's plan might somehow involve Meggy. So he wished them luck.

He and Mossy waved and called out their goodbyes as the wagon pulled away.

24.
Catsa

The two rode on silently for a time. When she couldn't hold it in any longer Rosette blurted out, "Oh, Mother Comfrey, *please,* tell me where we are going! Are we going to Meggy's? Am I going to sing for her?"

"Yes. Yes, my dear. I believe I have found a way for you to do just that. But you must be aware Rosette; this journey is not without some danger."

Rosette looked up at the old gnome with a steady gaze and after a moment said, "That's okay. I am not afraid. I just want to help Meggy."

"We have a distance to go today. When we stop later I will explain what we're going to do. Then you must take a nap so that you will be well rested! The task ahead of you could be very long and difficult. You will need as much rest as you can get."

When they arrived at the Commons Mother Comfrey steered Hasa towards the west where they passed under the arch of ferns and crossed Gus's bridge.

If Reader, you noticed that that was the *opposite* direction from Meggy's house, you would be correct. Mother Comfrey had her reasons to leave Limindoor Woods from that direction.

Once they had crossed the bridge and reached the meadow, they then turned north again following a well-worn path.

Mother Comfrey had so often traveled around that countryside on her way to help others that her wagon had worn many crisscrossing tracks in the open meadows. Tall Ones often mistook those wagon tracks for paths made by deer.

Having ridden up along the entire west side of the forest, Mother Comfrey then directed the wagon towards the east. (Reader, you might want to check the map on page 11 to follow their journey.)

She halted the wagon in the shadow of Star Mountain so that they might rest there a while until the evening. While Hasa was allowed to graze in the open meadow, Mother Comfrey spoke to Rosette about the task that lay ahead. She gave her specific instructions and repeatedly warned the mouse against taking any needless risks.

Certain that she fully understood her directions Mother Comfrey then suggested that Rosette go off to spend some time by herself. Soon the gentle melodies of the mouse's sweet song could be heard drifting across the field.

Before long Mother Comfrey called her to come into the wagon for her nap. And only when the sun started to set did she awaken her. "It is time for us to go on now. Are you rested enough, Little One?" she asked.

"Yes, Mother Comfrey. I believe so," Rosette said, yawning.

After harnessing Hasa to the wagon, Mother Comfrey lifted the mouse up to the seat and climbed up herself.

By the time they finally arrived at their destination it was already dusk. Mother Comfrey cautiously hid the wagon near Meggy's house, behind a high thicket of grass.

You should know that Mother Comfrey was very methodical (that means careful and orderly.) If this venture was to be successful, everything had to happen just a certain way.

The first thing she did was help Rosette out of her lovely sweater. (There was no way of knowing what conditions she would encounter on her journey, nor how tight the spaces that she'd have to squeeze through might be.)

Then she silently placed the mouse on the ground, kissed her and pointed her towards the back of the house.

Moments later, Mother Comfrey, with her basket into which she had earlier placed several bunches of dried herbs, went to sit on an exposed tree root. From there she had a good view of Meggy's front porch. As she sat there in the dark, she proceeded to slowly pluck the leaves off of the stems of an herb. And she waited.

And while Mother Comfrey waited, young Rosette was taking the first cautious steps of her perilous adventure to find Meggy.

You may recall that the main danger Mother Comfrey had warned Rosette of was the fact that Meggy's family kept a cat.

Many people now days have cats; cats who are very dear to them - cats who are greatly loved and admired for their affection and beauty. But in those days, cats often served another purpose. They worked. A cat was usually brought into a house to protect it from vermin ... in particular *mice* who were known to raid pantries and spoil the food. Unfortunately, Meggy's cat was such a cat.

Before you hear more about Rosette's adventures, it would be good to learn more about Meggy's cat.

Meggy's cat's name was Catsa. She was a sturdy tabby cat with a lovely snow white bib. She guarded the house against pests and in exchange was fed table scraps. And on cold evenings Catsa enjoyed a warm place before the hearth.

Now, let us go back to Mother Comfrey. The herb that Mother Comfrey was handling as she sat near Meggy's front door was called 'catnip'.

Have you heard of catnip? It belongs to the 'mint' family. Most cats find the scent of catnip just *irresistible*. (That means they can barely control their love for it.)

By plucking at the dried catnip Mother Comfrey was allowing its tempting scent to wind its way through the night air - all the way to Meggy's front porch.

In no time at all, Catsa caught that enthralling scent and was forcibly drawn to it. Can you imagine her surprise when she approached its source and found that she had been led to a *gnome*?

"Is that you, Cleo?" asked Mother Comfrey peering at the cat through the darkness. "My, my, it has been such a long time."

"*Me*-ow? No, my name is Catsa. My mother's name was Cleo," the cat replied to the strange gnome.

"Well, I am very pleased to meet you, Catsa. My name is Mother Comfrey. Your mother and I used to be friends. I guess it *has* been awhile since I have visited these parts."

"You are welcome here, Mother Comfrey. Any friend of my mother is a friend of mine," the cat replied very politely.

"Excuse me, Mother Comfrey! But, what, may I ask, is that delightful scent I smell?" inquired Catsa stepping even closer.

"What, you mean this?" asked the gnome waving the herb in front of the cat. "It is called catmint, or catnip. Here, you are welcome to some, if you like."

Reader, have you ever seen a cat with catnip? It can make them act very silly. Even cats who are generally very dignified will tumble about with great abandon in a very funny manner, rubbing their faces in the herb. That is exactly what Catsa did when Mother Comfrey placed a generous pile of catnip at her feet. She just could not help herself! She was simply *bewitched!*

Now, you must know, Reader, that Mother Comfrey, being a most loving Gentle-gnome, had *no* desire to make fun of Catsa. She would never be so unkind. She knew how cats loved catnip, so, in a way, she was giving Catsa much joy.

But, there was something else she was doing too. Have you figured it out yet? Yes, she was *distracting* the cat.

What did I say that farm cats did? They guard against mice. Can you guess what mouse Mother Comfrey wanted to keep Catsa from? Yes, indeed, our Little Rosette. By giving her that catnip, she hoped to keep Catsa *away* from the house and away from Rosette.

Now that Mother Comfrey, by distracting Catsa with the catnip, had made sure that there was *no* chance she'd be *in* the house for a while, you may finally learn what it was that Rosette was up to.

25.
The Climb

As soon as Rosette had left Mother Comfrey, she dashed as fast as she could towards the foundation of Meggy's house. The foundation of a house is where it connects to the ground.

Reader, you will be pleased to know that Rosette's mother had taken great effort to teach her how to make her way in life.

She had taught her that it was always safest for her if she stayed away from Tall Ones – as few Tall Ones cared for mice.

She had also been careful to teach her how to enter a Tall One's buildings, if it was ever necessary, for some reason to do so. The best way to get inside, she had explained, was to look for any opening along its foundation where wall board met with stone.

So that is just what Rosette did. She crept along the ground at the back side of the house until she discovered a very small gap, just as her mother had described. With some effort, she was able to only barely squeeze through it. (Isn't it good that she had removed her sweater earlier?)

Inside the wall, for that is where she had ended up, it was completely dark. Again, remembering her mother's training, the first thing she did was to become very still. She concentrated on using her *other senses*; her sense of touch and hearing and even smell. So, even though it was dark inside the wall, Rosette could "see" where she was. Besides using her tiny ears to *hear* with, she used her silky whiskers to *feel* and her little nose to *smell* her way. Her nose could also *sense* any differences in the temperature of the air.

Mother Comfrey had warned Rosette that there could be many unknown dangers ahead, even *without* the risk of a cat finding her. Rosette still had the scary task of navigating her way through an *unknown* maze of walls in order to find her way upstairs to Meggy's room. She would have to be so very careful! Rosette may have been taught how to get inside a home, but the rest of the journey would be up to her - her and her *inner strength*.

Only after many false starts did Rosette finally manage to climb up inside of the wall to the second floor where Meggy's bedroom was. Her lame foot added greatly to the challenge. When she got to the second floor she crawled about in the dark until she finally glimpsed the dim glow of candlelight shining through a small hole in the baseboard.

Somehow, she was able to squeeze through that opening too. And, as luck would have it, the opening brought her right into Meggy's room!

But now Rosette found that she was faced with an even greater difficulty. She was certain that she had found Meggy's bed because she could hear the girl's troubled breathing high above her. But the problem now was that Meggy was so very, very *high above* her.

Remember the trouble Rosette had climbing up onto Mossy's bed, that first night in Limindoor? Well, if you recall, Mossy's bed was a *gnome's* bed, and really not very high at all. But Meggy's bed, well, that was another matter. Meggy's bed was probably as high as *your* bed is Reader - which would be pretty high to a little mouse.

Whatever was she to do?

"Oh, no, I cannot fail now!" Rosette thought to herself, almost in tears, as she sat under the bed and peered up into the dimness high above her. "What do I do now? How can I ever get all the way up there and help Meggy?"

Then she remembered what Mother Comfrey had told her. Mother Comfrey had said that; she, Rosette, was *'more powerful than she could imagine'* and that there was *'only one mouse like her in the whole world.'* She told her that she was *'made of love'* and that she *'only had to listen inside her heart to find the answer to any question!'*

Rosette wasn't sure what that last thing really meant, but she decided to try it - because, at that moment she had no idea what to do next. So she sat completely still and waited and tried to *'listen inside her heart.'* She waited and waited.

Then suddenly something happened. Something that was, at once, both terrifying and fortunate! Meggy's mother entered the room!

She had come to check up on her daughter (though Rosette did not know that) *and* she had brought something with her. It was an afghan blanket.

Meggy's mama had wanted to be sure that her daughter was comfortable so she brought a beautiful, large, handmade blanket to spread over her sleeping child. The entire blanket was made up of many flower-colored squares. When Rosette ventured to peek, she saw in the dim glow of the lantern on the bedside table, that Meggy's bed looked as if it had suddenly become a blossoming garden.

Suddenly Rosette was aware of her danger. "What if she discovers me here?" she thought quickly scurrying back into the dusty shadows under the bed. "What should I do? Should I leave? No, if I leave, then this would have all been for nothing," she reasoned. "No, I must wait and *'listen inside my heart'*," she reminded herself.

So she stayed there and silently waited, trying to breathe evenly so that her heart would stop its pounding.

High above, Meggy's mother kissed her daughter and whispered to her that she loved her. Then she left the room, leaving behind that beautiful blanket… and what a blessing it was that she did.

26.
The Song

Rosette waited under Meggy's bed a bit longer, just to be sure that she was safe. Then she cautiously stepped out into the dim light.

When she looked up at Meggy's bed she literally squealed with joy. The length of that beautiful blanket cascaded all the way from the top of the bed *down to the floor.*

Because of the way it was made with spaces between the stitches, the blanket would serve as a magnificent *ladder* for Rosette!

"Oh, thank you, thank you!" she said sincerely. Who she was thanking we don't know… but we do know that her heart was bursting with gratitude!

Rosette studied the way the blanket draped in order to choose the best route to climb.

Yes, it would be a *very* long ascent. But as we know, Rosette was a determined mouse. And those open stitches in the yarnwork would make for a much easier climb than Mossy's simple blanket had offered.

Up and up she climbed, step by step. Although her lame paw was not hurting too much, it wasn't as strong as the others and so made for slow climbing.

"I can do it, I can do it," she told herself again and again as she climbed step over step. Although she was tiring with the climb she was determined.

"I love Meggy! I have a gift! Mother Comfrey believes in me! I can do this!" she repeated over and over to herself.

When she was almost half way up the blanket she was startled by the sound of a door banging downstairs. The sound so frightened her that she almost lost her grip and fell. "No," she told herself, "I *must* keep climbing. It can't be that much longer. It just can't be."

Still, up and up she climbed. Until, at last, she realized that she was no longer climbing *up*, but *across*, across the bed. She had made it!

As quickly as possible, she scurried towards Meggy's head.

Fortunately, Mother Comfrey had had the foresight to warn Rosette that Meggy was really a Tall One and that whenever she was *outside* of Limindoor Woods she would be the size of a *giant* and might not be recognizable.

"Oh, my, is that really Meggy?" Rosette wondered. "She is *enormous!*"

Rosette closed her eyes and sniffed. Yes, it was Meggy's smell. She knew it well. For ever since Meggy had given her that sweater the mouse had been embraced in that scent. It was a nice and comforting smell, kind of like flowers and also a bit like the buttery pastries that Meggy cooks.

Silently, Rosette stepped onto Meggy's pillow and walked closer to her head to peek to see if Meggy was awake. The child's eyes were closed and she was breathing irregularly.

Rosette paused there on the pillow. Now that she was finally there, she wondered about her song.

Would she be able to find the *right* song for Meggy? She knew how important that song would be - for Mother Comfrey had called her voice her 'gift' to give to others.

Rosette thought about the love she felt for Meggy and how very much she wanted Meggy to get well. She sat there and imagined Meggy all better again - healthy and smiling. She sat a moment longer and then finally she opened her little mouth and started to sing.

Sweet strains of the little mouse's wordless song sounded into Meggy's ear. They were so hushed they could hardly have been heard beyond the bed. But the notes were true enough to carry all of the magic that Rosette's love-filled heart could conjure. Rosette sang and sang.

When at long last her song came to an end she looked over at Meggy's face and saw that, although her eyes were still closed in sleep, her mouth had curved into a sweet smile.

"*Slam!*" She heard a door clap shut far downstairs. And then from a distance, she heard, "Catsa! Catsa! Here kitty, kitty, kitty. Where are you Catsa? It's supper time!"

Rosette crept up to Meggy's ear, gave her a kiss and whispered, "I hope you get better soon, Meggy!" Then she turned back to quickly start her descent down the blanket.

Fortunately, the way down took much less effort. A couple times when her grip slipped, her little sharp claws easily caught in the stitches and she was cushioned by the softness of the yarn.

Down to the floor, she scampered at last. And just as she slipped through the tiny opening in the wall she sensed that the door to Meggy's bedroom had opened again.

But it was no matter, for Rosette had done what she had come to do.

The way back down inside the walls was as dark as before, but the mouse was clever and she easily remembered the way.

In only moments she was standing outdoors, once again in the fresh chilly air of Meggy's back yard.

Mother Comfrey was waiting for her, confident of Rosette's success. She had brought the wagon around to the back of the house the moment that Catsa had gone indoors - for she intended to get underway as soon as Rosette appeared.

Quickly and silently, Mother Comfrey helped Rosette back into her little sweater to protect her from the frosty night air.

When they were finally settled on the wagon seat Rosette cuddled up to Mother Comfrey and said excitedly, "I *did* it, Mother Comfrey! I sang to her. I really *did* it!"

"Yes, dear one, I knew you would succeed," was Mother Comfrey's reply. "Thank you, Dear, Dear Rosette!"

Mother Comfrey tucked the soft mouse-sized blanket around Rosette who, after all of her many exertions, fell asleep at once.

The moon shone down on them with a soft honeyed light as Hasa silently pulled the wagon over the long road home.

The mouse didn't stir when they crossed Gus's bridge, nor when they got home at last and Mother Comfrey carried her to Mossy's door.

She didn't even awaken when Mother Comfrey handed her over to the sleepy old gnome and he tucked her into her cozy nest at the foot of his bed.

Mother Comfrey smiled with gratitude at Mossy before turning to leave.

Silently Hasa pulled Mother Comfrey's wagon along the night-shrouded path towards the Commons, while throughout Limindoor Woods all the gnomes lay snug in their beds dreaming their pleasant gnome dreams.

27.
Good News

The next day Gus waited eagerly by Apple Tree Hill for Meggy, hoping upon hopes that they could go to school together. He so hoped that somehow miraculously it had all been a bad dream and that Meggy hadn't been sick at all.

But after waiting far too long, he came to realize that it must sadly be true. Deciding to visit her at the end of the day, he sprinted off towards school and arrived only just before the school bell rang.

Meanwhile, back in Limindoor, Mother Comfrey, having slept the night in the Commons, had awakened early.

When Wren noticed her frost covered wagon sitting down there in the open she thoughtfully brought her a cup of hot tea.

While the two sat together in the snug wagon Mother Comfrey told her all about the previous night's adventures.

"She was quite remarkable, you know, that little white mouse. She was *fearless!* And she *did* finally succeed in singing to Meggy! I am only waiting now to find out if it worked," explained Mother Comfrey.

As they were talking, Mother Comfrey kept on peeking out of her caravan window. When at last she saw several birds flying about in the Commons she said to Wren, "Thank you again for the tea, my dear. Let's climb out now, for I must go ask a favor of Blue Bird."

All the creatures loved Mother Comfrey so much, that they would do anything for her. So when she asked Blue Bird to fly to Meggy's house and report back to her how Meggy was doing, the bird went off in a flash of blue.

By the time it took for Mother Comfrey to brush the morning dew off of Hasa's fur, Blue Bird returned bearing much news.

"Mother Comfrey," the bird twittered, "I did just as you asked me to do. I easily found Meggy's house but when I peered inside her upstairs window she wasn't there!"

"Not there, you say? Well, where was she?"

"I flew around and peeked into other windows until I saw someone in a room below. And when I flew to the windowsill I saw that it was Meggy! And she saw *me*!"

"Go on," said Mother Comfrey, now quite excited.

"When she opened the window… oh, such lovely smells came out! Meggy spread some yummy crumbs on the sill for me and wished me a sunny 'Good morning!' She seemed very cheerful!"

Mother Comfrey sighed with contentment. Rosette *had* succeeded. Her song *had* healed Meggy. How wonderful!

"Thank you so much, Blue Bird! Your news has made me very happy," she said.

Then she thought to herself, "I must return to Mossy's at once to tell Rosette!"

After quick 'goodbyes' to Blue Bird and Wren (who had also been thrilled by the good news since she too was very fond of Meggy), Mother Comfrey harnessed Hasa to the wagon.

She quickly climbed up and made her way south, smiling all the way.

28.
The Guardian

That same day, when school-time was over, at last, Gus was permitted to leave right away. He had explained his intention to check up on Meggy, so his teacher kindly excused him from his daily chores.

"Too bad it's not springtime so I could pick her some wildflowers," Gus thought to himself as he walked along. "Well, I'll bring her some of these pretty colored autumn leaves instead."

As a Gnome-in-training, Gus so enjoyed practicing being generous. He loved how good it felt when he made others smile by doing something nice for them.

A shortcut across Meggy's field brought Gus quickly to her front door. But, can you imagine how surprised he was when it was Meggy who answered his knock?

"Meggy! But, you are up! Are you all *better?*" he asked, astonished to see her standing there.

"Hi, Gus! Come on in. Yup, I am *all* better," she said dancing a little twirl. "I woke up sort of late this morning so mama kept me at home. I have been in the kitchen baking all day!"

As Gus stepped into the house he was surrounded by the delicious scent of Apple Jackets.

"I couldn't find any flowers so I brought you these," he said shyly handing the bouquet of colored leaves to her.

"Ooh, how pretty they are. I so love the autumn colors. Thank you. Do you want an Apple Jacket, Gus?"

What a silly question! Soon the children were sitting before the cheerful fire. Gus was licking his fingers having just enjoyed his *second* Apple Jacket. Meggy sat next to Gus and was about to tell him something important.

"Gus, now it's *my* turn to tell you about *my* dream. I had it last night and it too was *so* strange!"

"Was it about a bridge?" Gus asked with a grin.

"No, you silly," she said. "Now listen!

"I guess I had finally fallen asleep…I had been feeling pretty awful, you know. Ugh! My throat was so sore and my ear really ached.

"As I said, I was *sound asleep* and suddenly I dreamed that I heard the most beautiful singing…"

"Was it like Blue Bird's song, Meggy?" asked Gus, now quite interested.

"No, no! It was kind of like a voice – and yet, kind of *not*. I don't know. Actually, I think it sounded like an *angel* might sound."

"An *angel?*"

"Uh, huh," she nodded. "I don't remember any words. But, oh, it was *so beautiful.*

"And then I started to feel a golden light shining *deep* inside of me. And the light became brighter and brighter.

"I don't remember what happened next, but when I woke up this morning I didn't feel hot anymore. And *all* of my pains were gone too. Just like that! I am *all* better!" she grinned.

Gus sat there listening to her story in complete awe. "What do you mean, Meggy? Are you saying that an *angel* healed you?"

"I don't know, Gus," she said jumping up and spinning around the room. "But I do know I am not sick anymore. I am even going to go to school tomorrow!"

Gus was happy to hear that.

When, a moment later, Meggy asked Gus about the bridge, he said that he hadn't been back to see it yet but that Mother Comfrey had already *used* it.

"When I went to Limindoor to talk to Mother Comfrey about you, she had *just then* crossed the bridge. She said that she really liked it. She also said that it was Master

Kruk who had told her who had built it! Can you imagine that?"

Gus also mentioned to Meggy about seeing Mother Comfrey mysteriously take Mossy's mouse friend, Rosette, away with her in her wagon.

"Gus, you don't suppose that Mother Comfrey had something to do with my getting better, do you?"

"I don't know, Meggy. You've heard her voice when she sings. Did it sound like what you heard last night?"

"No, not at all. No, what I heard was not a gnome's voice, nor a person's. It was different – kind of *airy*."

"Besides," Gus continued. "How could Mother Comfrey get into your room, anyhow? She *is* a gnome you know. She's pretty small."

"No, you're right, Gus. Anyway, I still think it was an *angel* who sang to me... my *guardian* angel!"

The two sat and thought about what Meggy had just said. And they wondered.

Even though the two children were still quite young, they did know that sometimes you just had to 'wait for answers about things you don't understand.'

So after a moment they looked at each other, shrugged their shoulders and laughed.

"So, what did I miss in school today?" asked Meggy and Gus told her about all that had happened that day.

The two visited a bit longer and then Gus said 'goodbye' and promised to meet her on the path the next day.

29.
Autumn's End

The following days came and went. But by the next weekend, anyone visiting Limindoor would have surely felt the growing sense of expectation that was in the air.

Brother Acorn had started out early that morning. He knew that autumn was about to come to an end. He had lived through the changing of many seasons and was certain that winter was waiting for them just outside of Limindoor Woods.

Brother Acorn had a very important job to do - which was to be sure all the gnomes had stored *ample* firewood to fend off the winter's cold.

Yes, in case you are wondering, each gnome *did* have a tiny fireplace or stove in their home. How else could they heat their tea, cook their food, and keep toasty warm in the winter?

Ancient Gnome Wisdom had taught them how to build a place for a fire *inside* of a tree-trunk home, one that would in no way hurt the tree, yet would allow them to live there in comfort.

When Brother Acorn went from house to house and examined each gnome's wood pile, he was always pleased to see how each gnome had stacked their pile so neatly. You may recall that one of the Rules of Gnome is to keep tidy.

Mossy's task was to be sure that each gnome had enough dried moss for the winter ahead. This, each gnome stored in a hollow log that had been rolled into place near their home.

He too had been out and about since early that morning checking on everyone's log container. Of course, Mossy had brought along an extra bundle of moss with him, just in case someone's supply would need topping off.

Now, what do you think they used that moss for, Reader? Well, it was primarily used for stuffing their mattresses! The springy moss was so comfortable to sleep on and it smelled so good too. It was also used to help start their fires, as a kind of kindling. And, for really icy cold winters the gnomes knew it also served as a great insulator. When they stuffed moss inside their clothes (even their boots) it helped to keep them nice and warm.

With winter so close, it was Gilly's job to visit the gnomes to be sure that each had enough food stored.

For the last three seasons, Gilly had worked hard tending his wonderful garden. Since the garden was for *all* of Limindoor, other gnomes often came to help him work in it. In exchange, everyone had an abundance of vegetables, grains, fruit, nuts and seeds for their tables.

His task required that he enter each home to check the gnome's food storage. If he found that someone had forgotten to store some seeds or vegetables or something else he would have to take care of the problem.

Perhaps this is a good time to tell you something else about Gilly that most people didn't know. Gilly had a *secret*.

Late in the previous spring, Gilly had planted a special golden seed - one that Mother Comfrey had given him. (No, it was not a corn kernel.) That seed grew all summer long, hidden way in the back of his garden - a part of the garden that *no one* ever went to.

First, it grew into a plant with broad green leaves. Then it blossomed with a glorious golden star-shaped flower. And then that flower grew into a *Big Thing!* He kept the Big Thing hidden with lots of tall grasses growing around it so no one would discover it. If they had they probably wouldn't have said anything anyhow. You know how gnomes are, don't you?

You will not be hearing about the Big Thing again in this story, but for future reference, it is good to know that it was there.

Well, back to that particular autumn day. You can probably guess what Teasel and Tweed were up to. Had you walked by their place you would have heard the constant click-clicking of their knitting needles.

They were determined that every single gnome would have at least one new pair of socks that winter, and hopefully a pair of matching mittens as well.

They still had one last pair to make!

Pebble, you may be happy to hear, no longer climbed up Star Mountain that late in the year.

Once, when he was much younger and very eager about his work as a crystal gardener, he had managed to reach the top of the mountain *in the snow*.

But as soon as he got there he realized that he would never be able to find any star seeds in the glistening drifts anyway. And when he started to climb down the mountain on the snowy path, he slipped and, unable to stand up again, he skidded and slid all the way down the path on his *bottom!* Bump-bumpity-bump! My, he must have looked like a snow-gnome when he got home!

So, ever since, Pebble chose to devote those icy cold days to visiting with other the other gnomes of Limindoor Woods. That way he could catch up on all the news he had missed throughout the year.

As to his preparations for winter; Pebble would have had to scurry about gathering all the food, moss and firewood that he'd need before the cold came. But, because of the kindness of the other gnomes, they had all made sure that he had ample stores of everything.

That leaves us with one last gnome, Wren. As you know Wren's main contribution to the community was her music – well, that and her youthful spirit.

Wren always managed to cheer everyone up… not that they really needed it with Limindoor being such a happy place to live in. But sometimes the gnomes went about their lives as if in a dream - with each day being pretty much the same as the last.

Yet, when Wren showed up she would always surprise them with a smile or a tune on her flute. She was like a sunny day after it's been foggy for a while.

Another of Wren's tasks, self-appointed of course, was to look after the animals of Limindoor. She liked to check in on them to see if they were healthy and well fed, or if they needed anything.

She also was very attentive to the preparations the animals had made for the winter. Would they have enough to eat? Would they be warm enough?

Yes, the tasks, both daily and seasonal, were many, for those who lived in Limindoor Woods. They all took their responsibilities very seriously and in doing so made life there very agreeable.

30.
Winter

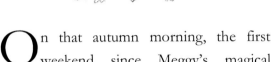

On that autumn morning, the first weekend since Meggy's magical recovery, the two children finally returned to Limindoor Woods.

Of course, Meggy's first stop was to see the Knitting Gnomes. But she was surprised to find that they were too busy with finishing the very last pair of socks they were knitting, to visit with her.

Gus had gone to visit Mossy but, after discovering that he was not at home he went to see Brother Acorn instead. When he arrived he found the old gnome struggling with Mossy's wheelbarrow. Brother Acorn was trying to deliver some last pieces of firewood to Pebble, so naturally, Gus helped him.

The whole forest felt like it was waiting for something very special that was about to happen.

And, where was Rosette in all of this commotion? She had gone to spend time in her Very Special Place in the Commons. However, when she'd arrived, she'd found Mother Comfrey's wagon parked nearby.

Mother Comfrey, it seems, had taken it upon herself to generously deliver acorn shells full of herbs to all of the gnomes. You know, of course, that she uses herbs to heal. But there are some herbs that make into lovely teas and others can be used to enhance the flavor of a nice vegetable stew.

Rosette was so happy when Mother Comfrey finally returned to her wagon.

"Hello Mother Comfrey," she said cheerfully as she scurried up to her.

"Why, hello Rosette! Would you like to come up into my wagon and get out of this cold for a while?"

"Ooh, yes, I'd like that!"

Even though Mother Comfrey's big herb basket was now empty, Mother Comfrey was surrounded with a cloud of beautiful smells. It was like she was wearing a summer meadow. "Gee, you smell nice, Mother Comfrey," said the mouse.

The old gnome smiled as she reached down and picked up Rosette. Then, just as she was helping the mouse inside her wagon, Meggy arrived.

"Oh, hi, Mother Comfrey! Isn't it exciting about winter coming?" said Meggy cheerfully.

"Hello, Meggy! Indeed it is. Say, Meggy, Little Rosette is here in my wagon. I know these are close quarters, but would you like to come in for a visit, too?"

"Oooh, thank you. I would love to. I have never been *inside* of your wagon before," she said as she climbed up. "Hello, Rosette. I haven't seen you in a long time."

Rosette smiled shyly and looked up at Mother Comfrey for a clue as to what to say. For, even though Meggy had *not seen*

Rosette that night, Rosette had certainly *seen* Meggy!

"I understand that you were recently very ill Meggy," said Mother Comfrey. "I am so glad to see you are all well again,"

"I was. And I *am* all better now," said Meggy. "And I think it is all because of my guardian angel!"

"Your *guardian angel?*" asked a very surprised Mother Comfrey.

"Yes!" said Meggy excitedly to the both of them.

Then she proceeded to tell them about the dream she had had that night – about the beautiful singing and the golden light she had felt grow inside her – and how she was so sure that it could have been none other than her guardian angel.

Mother Comfrey smiled warmly at Meggy and said, "Meggy, I think that you should know who that guardian angel was so that you might thank her."

"What? Thank her?" said Meggy, clearly not believing her ears. "What do you mean, Mother Comfrey?"

Mother Comfrey turned to Rosette and asked, "May I tell her?"

Poor Rosette! Could she have turned any pinker? "Alright, Mother Comfrey," she whispered.

"Dear Meggy, I am certain that you *do* have a special Guardian Angel who watches over you at all times. But you should know that your Guardian Angel had a special helper the other night when you were so very sick. It was our Dear Little Rosette here who was that helper.

"You see, Rosette has a very special gift. It is her voice. Our Rosette, here, *sings*. And very special songs they are, too."

"You mean to say it was *you* who was singing to me, Rosette?" said Meggy, totally astonished.

"Yes, dear, it was Our Rosette here, who, filled with love, and at great risk, made it *all the way* up to your room, *all the way* to your pillow, so that she might sing to you."

Upon hearing that Meggy's eyes started to tear up with gratitude for the little mouse.

But before she could thank her a great *CLANGING* sound filled the air.

Someone was ringing the Ding-Dong!

Although Meggy was still stunned by Mother Comfrey's news, the racket the gong made was very demanding.

So demanding, in fact, that the three 'ladies' decided to exit the wagon to see what was happening.

Meggy quickly took Rosette up into her arms, said something into the mouse's ear and gave her a hug. And as it was so cold she decided to carry the mouse as they rushed off to see what the fuss was all about.

In response to the sound of the gong, all of the gnomes, Gnomes-in-training, and creatures of Limindoor Woods, had gathered into the Commons as well.

It was Mossy who had rung the alarm. He was still holding onto the great metal spoon he used for that purpose and was waving it in the air with a big smile on his face.

"Welcome, my friends!" he called out. "We did it! We finished *all* the Work of Autumn. And it was a job well done, too!

"And, I might add, just in time.

"For now, ta-da, it is officially *winter*!"

A great cheer of 'Hurrah' rose from the crowd. There were hugs and pats on backs. Any birds who were present flew about in great loops. The squirrels did some joyous acrobatics and Hasa's strong hind legs made a few jubilant thumps on the ground.

The gnomes all came into a circle and started singing.

♪ "We give thanks, we give thanks, for *our work now done*. Autumn is gone; winter is here, so let's enjoy the cold." ♪

And then, as if on cue, it started to *snow!* First, one solitary snow flake fluttered down. Then a second one and soon others followed softly, silently, resting on the ground.

Gus and Meggy were utterly astonished. To all the others, they were the same beautiful snowflakes that fell in Limindoor Woods every winter. But for Gus and Meggy well, they had never seen, never imagined, flakes of that size. They were almost the size of saucers. And each flake was a wonder of lacy white delicacy. The two were transfixed with the beauty that surrounded them.

"Well, my friends. Off we go - home to get warm. Thank you all for the generous work you did. It is because of each and every one of you that this is sure to be a *snug and comfortable* winter for us all!"

Then Mossy sang another song. (The music to this is on page 224.)

♪ "Thank you, Thank you, Thank you very much. Thank you very much!" ♪

Each of the others joined in, singing the same song, but this time together as a round (that is when everyone sings the same words but joins into the song at a different time.)

♪ "Thank you, Thank you, Thank you very much. Thank you very much!" ♪

Soon everyone in all of Limindoor was glowing with gratitude!

Limindoor Woods is all quiet now, covered in a soft blanket of white. Every gnome and creature is snug in their home, all cozy and warm.

Gus and Meggy are in their homes too, probably curled up in front of their fireplaces gazing into the flames.

Perhaps they are thinking about all their friends in Limindoor and wondering how the winter will be for them.

Perhaps they are thinking of how much fun they will have being the size of the gnomes when enjoying a winter in Limindoor Woods.

Perhaps they are thinking about how grateful they are to have found Limindoor Woods - grateful for the magic they have experienced there, and grateful for all of their good friends.

"Stars and moon and sun,
Now this story's done."

Things to Ponder

- The Way of Gnome 221
- Music for the Gnome Songs 224
- The Gnomes give Thanks 225
- Gratitude Soup Recipe 227
- About Mice 231
- How to make Acorn-Cap Candles 234
- About the Author 239
- In Gratitude 241

The Way of Gnome

If you have read the other Tales of Limindoor Woods you have certainly come across what is called 'The Way of Gnome.'

The Way is a collection of rules, or guides, for gnomes to live by – rules that gnomes learn and follow when they are very young. The gnomes are taught that if they follow these basic tenants they are sure to become very happy Gentle-gnomes.

Since the Tales of Limindoor Woods are now being shared outside of Limindoor, it seems that more and more Tall Ones are also finding great benefits from learning and following 'The Way of Gnome.'

The rules are as follow:

1. **Be Kind**: Always.

2. **Tell the Truth**: Always, and if you feel you can't, it is best to say nothing. (You might want to ask your parents about this.)

3. **Be Generous**: Always offer a gift when you meet someone. If you don't have a gift, sing a song, tell a story or give creatively in some other way. Even a smile or hug will do.

4. **Keep Tidy**: It is mainly a matter of keeping things in order and clean. Do the best you can while still having fun.

5. **Celebrate Every Day**: Do this in some way, even if you are by yourself; for each day is a *wonder*. You can sit still, enjoy beauty, appreciate something or someone, or just feel gratitude.

The Sixth Rule

Only when the five main rules become part of your very nature do you learn the Sixth Rule.

The Sixth Rule says that once you become a Gentle-gnome you should discover what your *Gift* is.

What is that special thing that you love to do? What is that thing that you can do very well? For that probably is your Gift.

What do we do with Gifts? We give them away.

The gnomes believe that the main reason they are alive is so that they can give their gift to others.

What do you think your gift is?

Music for Songs

Make New Friends

We Give Thanks

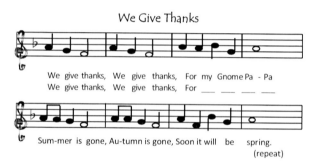

Thank You Song

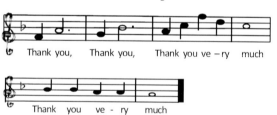

The Gnomes Give Thanks

It is a tradition that each gnome sings their own unique verse of the Gratitude Song at the Gnomes' Thanks-Giving Celebration.

That way everyone can learn what their fellow gnomes are most thankful for. And after they sing their verse, the entire group echoes what they sang. Since there are quite a few gnomes in Limindoor their songs can go on for quite a while.

Here are the different things that each gnome said at this Gnomes' Thanks-Giving Celebration that they were grateful for.

Maybe before reading the following, it might be fun for you to guess what you think they might have said.

1. Mother Comfrey gave thanks for the healing herbs.
2. Brother Acorn gave thanks for the healthy trees.
3. Mossy gave thanks for having known his friend Mees.

4. Gilly sang his thanks for Hummy Bee. (Since Hummy Bee was *not* at the festivities, she didn't hear Gilly's praise. She was, in fact, in the Royal Hive with her beloved Queen. But all present at the celebration knew how very important she and all of the bees were to the health of Gilly's garden - the source of *all* of the gnomes' sustenance. So they all promised to thank her when next they saw her.)
5. Pebble gave his thanks for the Star Seeds that grew into crystals.
6. & 7. Teasel and Tweed sang with one voice and gave thanks for the sheep's warm wool.
8. Wren gave thanks for all the sweet songs from the birds.
9. Gus gave thanks for his dear Gnome-papa, Mossy.
10. Meggy sang of her thanks for the Kitting Gnomes. (Many months before, the Kitting Gnomes, Teasel and Tweed, had assisted Meggy with her knitting and so they had become such good friends.)

Gratitude Soup Recipe

Have you ever made soup before? It is really quite easy.

This soup is made collaboratively. That means it takes several people to work together to make it. It's more fun if a number of people add their favorite vegetables to the pot.

This recipe makes about 8 servings. If you are making soup for more, you can double the amounts. You can make less by dividing the amounts, but why not have some left over? Leftover soup can taste so good the next day.

The first items on the list of ingredients are pretty necessary to make the soup really tasty.

Necessary Ingredients

- 6 cups broth (vegetable or chicken)

To make the vegetable broth from scratch, simply simmer vegetable scraps and some herbs (parsley, thyme or bay) in water for about 45 min. Then strain the liquid and use it

To make the chicken broth from scratch, boil up to 3 lb. of all parts of the chicken, with onion, celery, pepper and herbs (parsley, thyme or bay) for 2 hours. Spoon off any foam that might arise in the pot. And then strain the liquid and use.

- 1 Tbsp. butter, olive or vegetable oil
- 1 medium onion (chopped) and/or
- 1 large clove of garlic (chopped)
- Salt & pepper
- Herbs such as parsley, thyme or bay

Contributions

Whoever is contributing to the soup can choose from these optional ingredients:

- 2 stalks of celery ribs (chopped fine)
- 1-2 carrots (sliced into coins)
- 2-3 leaves flags of greens such as kale, chard, spinach, collards (chopped)
- Up to a cup green peas or chopped green beans
- Up to a cup corn kernels
- Yellow squash (diced)
- Zucchini (diced)
- Red bell pepper (chopped)
- 2-3 medium potatoes (chopped, skins on)
- 2 cups pasta, rice or other grains (precooked)
- Can you think of other vegetables to use?

Directions:

Parents/Guardians, please attend your little ones as this requires knives & a hot stove.

1. If making the soup *with a grou*p, be sure that each person has brought one or more of the ingredients.
2. Melt butter or heat oil in a LARGE pot and sauté onion
3. (and/or garlic) on medium-high for 2-4 minutes until golden.
4. Stir in the firmer of the chopped vegetables, sautéing for 6-8 minutes.
5. Then pour the broth (vegetable or chicken) into the pot.
6. Heat until boiling.
7. Add the softer vegetables and the cooked grains or pasta.
8. Cook a while longer.
9. Season to taste with salt & pepper and any spices you like.
10. Ladle into individual bowls.
11. Give thanks for the bounty shared by all and enjoy the soup!

About Mice

Mice are such curious creatures. They are so tiny that many people find them charming.

But there also are many people who are frightened of them as well. If you can believe it, there are even stories about huge elephants being frightened of mice. Perhaps it is the speed with which the mice scurry about that is most alarming to both people and elephants.

Here are some interesting facts about mice that you might not have known.

Some mice, when full grown, are only an *inch* long, whereas others can grow to be as large as *seven* inches long. My, what a large mouse that would be!

Mice are usually nocturnal (that means they are awake at night); that is unless they live in Limindoor. Because their eyes are not particularly strong they have to depend on other senses, like their ears and nose.

Their whiskers can sense temperature changes as well as the texture of any surface they touch.

Mice are generally very good jumpers (unlike little Rosette who was, you may remember, a bit lame). They are also quite nimble and can get through the smallest openings.

Did you know that besides climbing and jumping, mice can also swim?

Generally, mice rarely live to be *two* years old in the wild (as there are so many predators there.) Few mice live to be four years old, even in captivity. That the mouse, Mees, lived to be as old as he was must have had something to do with the magic of Limindoor Woods.

As to mice singing, that actually is a *fact*. Mice *do* sing.

However, it is usually a male mouse who sings to charm a lady mouse. And the songs are pitched so high that they are hardly discernable to the human ear.

Again, you should remember Reader that any gnome or creature who lived in Limindoor must have had some pretty strong magic.

That being so, might explain why Rosette had such a unique voice.

You might also be surprised to learn that mice are known to purr. Their purr sounds a bit more like a repeating click than the low vibration of a cat's purr.

How to Make Acorn-cap Candles

If you would like to make your own acorn-cap candles, be advised that, unless *you are of gnome size*, it is preferable that they *only* are lit when they are floating in a bowl of water. Generally, the size of a Tall One's hands is just too big to be able to safely hold a lit acorn-cap candle.

Please read through the instructions *first* before starting.

There are a couple ways to make these.

1.) For the easiest way you will need:

   1. A large beeswax candle
   2. A spoon
   3. Candle wick (available at craft stores) 1" per candle
   4. A number of clean, *thoroughly dry* and *un-cracked* acorn caps
   5. A plate or tray filled with a ½" layer of dried grains (rice, millet, or the like) or sand

2.) Or another method

(one requiring a stove)

1. A large sauce pan
2. Either a glass measuring cup with a hooked handle **or** a clean tin can
3. Beeswax bits (You can save your old candle stubs for this. Of course, beeswax is what the gnomes would have used, but if you only have paraffin wax that will work too… as will old bits of crayons!)
4. Candle wick (available at craft store) 1" per candle
5. A number of clean, *thoroughly dry* and *un-cracked* acorn caps
6. A plate or tray filled with a ½" layer of dried grains (rice, millet, or the like) or sand

Directions

1.) The simplest way to create these tiny candles is to light a large beeswax candle and wait until melted wax pools around the wick.

Spoon up some of the melted wax and drop a few drops into the bottom of an acorn cap. Hold an end of a cut wick piece into the melted wax until the wax hardens, 'gluing' it in place. Then bend the wick up so it stands upright in the cap. Place cap in the grains or sand to hold upright and spoon in more melted wax to fill the cap.

When the wax solidifies, trim the wick to ½".

2.) A more complex manner of making these requires the stove.

Break up your wax into small pieces and place in a glass, hook handled, measuring cup, or a clean tin can. Place the vessel into water that is heating in a saucepan to melt the wax.

Carefully spoon up some of the melted wax and drop a few drops into the bottom of an acorn cap. Hold an end of a cut wick piece into the melted wax until the wax hardens, 'gluing' it in place. Then bend the wick up so it stands upright in the cap. Place cap in the grains or sand to hold upright and spoon in more melted wax to fill the cap.

When the wax has solidified, trim the wick to ½".

The safest way to enjoy these little candles is to float them in a bowl or cup of water.

Aren't they delightful?

About the Author

Always a dreamer, I linger in that magic 'in-between space', where fairytales, fantasy, and the marvels of nature color my experience of life – the magic place of 'wonderment.'

As a child, living among artists, I was given freedom to explore a variety of art mediums. I was encouraged to find new ways to express myself and my imaginings. And in a Waldorf school, I was able to experience the many diverse and rich facets of a holistic education.

As an adult, I returned to Waldorf to receive a graduate degree as a Waldorf teacher. Now, after many happy years of kindergarten and classroom teaching, both in the States and in Italy, I am retired. I am pleased to add that several of my students have gone on to become teachers themselves.

During the years I taught I also experienced the joy of being a parent of two wonderful, creative children. And at present rejoice in the delights of being a grandmother of four.

Now, at last, I have the time to be still, to find inspiration from nature, to enjoy the company of my dear husband and our cat, to write, to travel and to daydream.

Please visit me at teachwonderment.com

In Gratitude

For their love, guidance, inspiration, encouragement, for fostering my imagination and creativity, for identifying my relationship with wonderment, for introducing me to the elementals, and for allowing me to dream…

I thank my dear mother, Tree McGarrity, my beloved boys, Joseph and Gus, my Artist Godmother, Mary Shore, my Fairy Godmother, Ella Young, my teachers, Ted De Grazia and Lee Lecraw.

And to those who continue to make my days ever bright: I thank my beloved husband, James Guzzetta, my precious daughter, Cristalla, my four cherished grandchildren, Coy, Gus, Shane and Liberty Rose, my son-in-law, Ben, my dear friends, Shirley, Wiebke, Liz, Toni, Jill and Marie and many other good friends who have nourished my spirit over the years.

Love and blessings, to *all* of you friends; you are all so dear to me.

Likewise, my love and blessings go to all the children who now grace our world and those who are on the way. May you know the world through eyes of wonderment!

And, last of all; let me not forget to thank the gnomes.

I am so grateful that they continue to whisper their numerous stories to me. Every Limindoor gnome has a special place in my heart. And I consider it a great honor to pass their tales on to the world.